"Not Bad, But You're Holding Your Back Too Stiff."

Kate spun around, only to find her worst nightmare realized. She was brushing up on her dance steps in supposed solitude, only to find Giles Channing standing not more than a few yards away. He casually leaned against the stable wall. His words, as well as the smile on his face, clearly indicated he'd seen enough to humiliate her completely. She wanted to sweep up her skirts and run. Instead she lifted her chin, determined to brazen it out.

"Lost your way to your car, Mr. Channing?"

He tore his gaze from the appealing—too appealing—picture she made and considered his surroundings. Actually, he *had* been contemplating leaving. Bored, he'd stepped out to the veranda to indulge in a smoke and consider his options. Then he'd spotted the light on in the stable.

"No," he said, returning his gaze to her. "I found what I was looking for. You promised me a dance, Katherine."

In the dim light of the single lamp, his classical features were even more striking. She'd never had a problem holding her own with anyone, but he managed to make her feel naïve and awkward.

"As I'm sure you've already noticed," she began coolly, "it's not one of my favorite activities."

With a shrug, he moved away from the wall and stepped closer. "Dancing, like riding and making love, is something that requires the right partner to do it well. Would you like me to show you?"

Dear Reader:

Welcome to Silhouette Desire—sensual, compelling, believable love stories written by and for today's woman. When you open the pages of a Silhouette Desire, you open yourself up to a new world—a world of promising passion and endless love.

Each and every Silhouette Desire is a wonderful love story that is both sensual *and* emotional. You're with the hero and heroine each and every step of the way—from their first meeting, to their first kiss... to their happy ending. You'll experience all the deep joys—and occasional tribulations—of falling in love.

In future months, look for terrific Silhouette Desire romances from some of your favorite authors, such as Annette Broadrick, Dixie Browning, Nancy Martin and Lass Small, just to name a few.

So go wild with Desire. You'll be glad you did!

Lucia Macro
Senior Editor

HELEN R. MYERS

KISS ME KATE

SILHOUETTE *Desire*

Published by Silhouette Books New York

America's Publisher of Contemporary Romance

SILHOUETTE BOOKS
300 East 42nd St., New York, N.Y. 10017

ISBN: 0-373-05570-6

First Silhouette Books printing May 1990

Printed in the U.S.A.

HELEN R. MYERS

says she knew Giles Channing was special from the moment he appeared in her most recent Desire, *The Pirate O'Keefe*. "Anyone who could hold his own against the pirate had to be. But making him settle down was another story. You can imagine my relief and enthusiasm when I found the one woman who could rattle such a charming sophisticate. How fitting that the earl with no earldom should be felled by a rather tart variety of Georgian peach. All this time he'd believed peaches were simply sweet. What lessons he'll be able to teach his sons!"

To Sandra Shipman at The Book Inn
Tyler, Texas

A kind lady
A gentle friend
A terrific bookseller

This one's for you.

One

The limousine left the city limits of Atlanta and wove its way through the gently rolling hills of the Piedmont Plateau, seemingly on a chase after the sinking sun. Black and sleek, it was in fact involved with an undertaking—and running late. Even so, Giles Channing sat in the back seat and observed the passing scenery with the casual interest of a man who didn't seem concerned that he should have reached his destination a half an hour ago.

A small herd of horses raced across a lush green pasture, luring a smile to his lips. The rolling terrain and spirited animals reminded him of another place, his ancestral home in northern England and, for a moment, he felt an uncharacteristic though fleeting surge of loneliness.

Maybe he should have gone back for a visit before taking on this newest venture. July was splendid in Westridge. Besides that, his nieces and nephews were growing so quickly; and hadn't his sister-in-law and brother threatened to take down his portrait in the family gallery if he didn't start showing up more often?

But when restlessness had struck, prompting him to leave Big Salt Island and his friends Garret and Laura O'Keefe, to buy up Garret's interest in Orion Development International and strike out on his own again, he'd ended up in the States instead. Laura had all but boxed his ears for leaving just before Garret Jr.'s first birthday party; however, it couldn't be helped. Giles had won the contract to build Theodore Beaumont's multimillion-dollar hotel and entertainment complex in downtown Atlanta, and a coup often demanded its own price. Yet how he allowed himself to get talked into donning this regalia and attending Teddy's Fourth of July costume ball to celebrate the project's ground-breaking was beyond him.

"Americans," he mused, tucking a finger between his white-on-white madras cravat and high-necked shirt. Their almost childlike zeal to celebrate that which hadn't yet been proven never failed to amuse him. One would think the celebration should come after the successful completion of Beaumont Center. But knowing Teddy—as Giles was just beginning to—one would no doubt follow that, as well.

"What's that, boss?" the driver asked, taking his eyes off the road to study him in the rearview mirror for what seemed an inordinately long period of time.

Giles thought it a commendable achievement to be able to meet the driver's curious inspection without exposing any concern, when the likelihood of their mating with one of those majestic oaks dotting the roadside was becoming more probable with every passing moment. O'Keefe would have enjoyed a daredevil like this, at least the O'Keefe of years past would. Giles himself had a more circumspect approach to his existence; until someone came back from the other side with proof in advertising, he would just as soon stay alive.

"I was merely admiring the scenery," he drawled, doing so again. They sped past a hawk perched on a fence post eyeing something in the tall grass. As they passed, the bird's feathers flew every which way, leaving it looking more than a little disheveled. "How much farther to the Beaumont estate?" Giles added resignedly.

"Two miles, as the crow flies, five for us 'cause we gotta go around that hill up ahead. Say, you ain't from these parts, are you? I can tell by your accent."

"I see Mr. Beaumont hired you for more than your instinctive driving abilities."

"Mr. B. likes to get to where he's going. You Australian?"

Giles lifted an eyebrow and this time settled his gaze on the back of the driver's head and the chauffeur's cap that rested at a jaunty angle. "English."

The driver shrugged in a way that suggested he thought the difference negligible. "You know what you need to make that outfit look right? A little blood right here." With his finger, he drew a line downward from the right side of his mouth.

Giles uncrossed his legs and leaned forward slightly, not sure he'd heard correctly. "Good Lord, whatever for?"

"Because that's what everybody does to make Count Dracula look realistic."

"I see." Giles leaned back in his seat again and reached into his coat for one of his long, slim cigars. Dear Laura, ever the conscientious physician, had been after him to cut down, but at the moment he needed the temporary panacea. "Thanks for the advice, but I'm going as his cousin, Monte Cristo," he drawled.

The driver's expression went from confused to disappointed. "I guess I ain't never heard of him."

Giles rolled the cigar between his fingers before lighting it and decided the evening could only improve. However, even the prospect of reacquainting himself with Teddy's eldest daughter failed to lift his waning spirits.

Not that Elizabeth wasn't lovely, he thought, remembering the elegant blonde who'd accompanied her father to their luncheon when Giles arrived earlier in the week. But ice maidens had never inspired more than an aesthetic appreciation in him. He did, however, have to allow that the lady was only recently widowed, which could explain the wall of reserve he'd sensed she kept around herself. He could only imagine what the other daughter was like. For some reason he couldn't remember, she hadn't joined her sister and father that day.

So much for his old friend O'Keefe's teasing that he might finally meet his match in a genteel Southern beauty...though there had been that comely brunette checking into the suite next to his when he'd left the hotel. Her clothes had said Paris, her smile said interested; it was something to remember in the off chance he saw the opportunity to make a discreet exit from Teddy's party.

"That white board-and-brick fence up ahead marks the beginning of Meadowbrook," the driver said, breaking into Giles's thoughts.

Giles viewed a sizable peach orchard beyond the fence, a stone-and-mortar bridge built over a lazily flowing creek and beyond that, a sprawling pasture dotted with a number of horses, any of which promised to make a challenging mount. He'd often dreamed of establishing his own stables but the restlessness that had originally led him from England had also turned him into a nomad of sorts. It was his older brother Richard's destiny to be the landowner, not his, and as the Earl of Westridge, Richard was up-holding tradition admirably.

Not that Giles had any regrets by any means. Now thirty-six, he could readily say the years of globetrotting had been as entertaining as they'd been profitable; and as the limousine sped past the crystal clear creek, he felt confident that the best was yet to come.

The driver turned the limousine through wrought-iron gates and they drove down a razor-straight drive lined with pecan trees that resembled giant sentries keeping a watchful eye over whoever passed below. The endless number of other limousines and cars also lining the driveway confirmed their lateness.

Finally the house itself appeared, a veritable light at the end of a tunnel. Gas lamps, already lit, circled the rounded portion of the drive by the house and the walkway leading to the steps. Added to the amber hue of sunset, they illuminated the white, two-storied structure with an ethereal glow that made Giles wonder if stepping from the limousine would mean stepping back in time.

He smiled at the fanciful thought as the car slid to a halt before a formally-dressed footman whose gold satin waistcoat made him look like an oversized firefly. Giles crushed out his cigar in the ashtray. At any rate, he concluded, Teddy went all out when it came to throwing a party.

"Evening, suh," the attendant said as Giles stepped from the vehicle and adjusted his cape. "They're expecting you. Go right on in."

Nodding, Giles walked up the sidewalk wishing it was still spring so he could see the heralded azaleas and magnolias in bloom. Then, too, he might not be feeling like a lobster in a boiling pot, he thought drolly as the effects of the sultry heat sent the first trickle of sweat down his spine.

He could only hope the house was as well air-conditioned as the car had been. But when he heard the music drifting out though the tall opened windows, he indulged in another sigh of resignation.

Along the pillared veranda Uncle Sam walked arm in arm with Cleopatra and farther down a lion sat on a swing sipping champagne with Elizabeth I. Feeling slightly less ridiculous than he had when he'd left the hotel, Giles climbed the front stairs and went inside.

Just beyond the front door was another attendant. Giles gratefully relinquished his cape to him. But before Giles could ask about his host, Teddy Beaumont stepped from the ballroom into the foyer and called to him in a bellowing voice that, despite the music and conversation already filling the house, overwhelmed it like thunder.

"Channing! I was about to send out a search party for you."

"My apologies." Giles accepted his host's beefy outstretched hand and the hearty backslap that accompanied it. Though he offered no other explanation, his smile was friendly.

He liked the rough-edged Southerner, who looked more like a bouncer than a businessman. Appearances aside, Teddy was one of the state's greatest success stories. Having amassed his fortune through shrewd business dealings, he'd solidified his position in Georgia society by marrying the only child of one of the oldest families in the state. Yet he remained unspoiled and Giles found him wonderfully uncomplicated. Teddy worked hard and drank hard, but the widower was clearly and disarmingly devoted to his two daughters.

"Seems like a lot of folks are running late tonight," Teddy grumbled, running a hand over the front of his confederate officer's uniform, stretching dangerously against the ample protuberance of his belly. "I was just about to go upstairs and see what's keeping— Why here she comes now. Katy, darlin'!"

Giles turned, curious to see who could wipe a scowl off his new business associate's face so quickly and found himself experiencing a myriad of emotions, predominantly amusement. A young woman was descending the double-width staircase, a vision of loveliness in her gold-and-white gown. But if her demeanor was anything to go by, "Katy darlin'" didn't appear to be in the best frame of mind to attend any party.

She stomped down the stairs—no easy feat, Giles noted, considering the yards of material that had been invested in creating her costume—while viciously tugging at the camisole exposed by the elbow slashings on the gown's sleeves. With every step she took, her long, pale hair lifted off her bared shoulders like a moon-kissed cloud floating in a night breeze. But the enchanting vision was fractured by her mutinous expression.

"Damned fine mess," Giles heard her mutter under her breath in a voice that currently held only a trace of the sweet, melodious tones he'd come to savor in Southern women since his arrival. "Who ever heard of wearing brocade in July! I must've been out of my mind to let her choose a costume for me."

Teddy, seemingly oblivious to her fussing, beamed proudly at Giles. "That's my baby."

Teddy's "baby" parked herself on the last stair so that father and daughter stood eye to eye. The better for her to glare, Giles noted, narrowing his own eyes with growing interest. She was small and reed slender, and her eyes were an exquisite clear blue—but hardly demure. Giles suddenly had the feeling his preconceived notions about

Southern belles was about to undergo some rapid modifications.

"Daddy, I'm not going in there like this," Kate Beaumont announced. The declaration was accented by the steady drumbeat of her short, unpolished nails tapping on the mahogany banister and caused a look of sheer bafflement to replace the welcoming smile on Teddy's face.

"But why not, kitten? You look beautiful."

"This thing weighs a ton and it's damned hot!"

"Now, Katherine, you know how I feel about unladylike language for my girls."

"And will you look at this mess?" she continued, ignoring her father's patient rebuke to once again pluck at her sleeve. "It's ripped at the elbows. Where's Elizabeth? It's bad enough that you've insisted I attend this silly ball, she could at least have made sure the costume she rented for me was wearable!"

Giles cleared his throat and stifled a smile. "Excuse me, Miss Beaumont, but if I'm not mistaken, slashings in the sleeve were considered the style back then. This is a Renaissance era gown, isn't it? My guess would be—Venetian?"

Kate considered the dark-haired man standing beside her father. In her agitated state she'd barely noticed him before, but now that she did she wished she hadn't. Not only did she have to look up another inch or two to meet his strange pale green eyes, but she didn't think she cared for the laughter she saw twinkling in their depths.

All her life she'd had to fight to be taken seriously by her father's peers, most of whose philosophies dated back to the dinosaurs. They all thought she should have been content with cotillion balls and now ladies clubs, or better yet, raising another generation who saw no harm in treating their women as if they were little more than pretty dolls.

Occasionally, she could tolerate the verbal pat on the head from her father, because as dinosaurs went, at least he was a darling; but she would be damned if she would be patronized by a—a *foreigner*.

"And who are you?" she asked with a deceptive sweetness as she extended her hand. "Wait. Let me guess." His accent was English, she decided, giving his long lean body a cool inspection. His black formal wear, though irreproachably tailored, was simple, his waistcoat unembroidered and like his madras cravat, white. Costume or not, she read "establishment" and that only fueled her agitation. "I know—you're one of the dreaded bankers for this planned albatross of my father's, or the attorney, perhaps?"

Before Teddy could do more than sputter incredulously, Giles broke into an easy grin and, taking her hand, lifted it to his lips. "The dreaded developer, I'm afraid. Giles Channing at your service, Miss Beaumont."

For an instant she simply stared at his raven-black hair. It wasn't the first time someone had turned what was meant to be a handshake into a kiss; it was, however, the first time that her skin tingled in reaction. But before she had time to wonder why, she caught him watching her and knew he was aware he'd thrown her off balance. What's more, he was enjoying it.

Kate snatched her hand back and met his assured smile with a more frigid one of her own. "I thought Orion Development International was going to do the project? Don't tell me the infamous Garret O'Keefe let you outbid him?"

"In a manner of speaking. I bought him out."

That gave her a moment's pause. It had been bad enough to learn that Orion had won the contract to handle her father's latest venture—anyone who kept up with newspaper headlines knew O'Keefe was a formidable power on any level—but to learn that even O'Keefe could be bought out .... It made her earlier confidence in herself and in her belief that the project could be stopped take a stomach-rolling nosedive.

"How nice for you," she managed stiffly.

"We're lucky to have him as our guest on two counts," Teddy injected, sending her a look of appeal. "Giles is also the brother of the Earl of Westridge."

"Imagine that," Kate drawled. "And here I thought the purpose of the Revolutionary War was to rid ourselves of the aristocracy."

Teddy's face turned the color of his uniform, but Giles merely lifted his eyebrow and glanced around his impressive surroundings. There was no doubt that the lovely Katherine had been raised in privilege, but it was becoming increasingly clear she preferred raising hell. "So they say," he murmured agreeably. "Odd thing, too. Why bother go through all that trouble—only to replace them with an aristocracy of your own?"

Before she could respond, he raised his hands in surrender. Candlelight flickered along the satin of his waistcoat, in his eyes and hair, and for a fleeting moment Kate thought of panthers gliding through a dark jungle, at one with the night. It gave her the oddest impulse to run back upstairs and lock her bedroom door.

"As you can see, Miss Beaumont, *I* came unarmed, and to further rest your mind, the title is solely my brother's, thank God. But be assured that I spoke with him only last week, and he made no mention of any plans to launch an assault on your fair shores."

At that moment Elizabeth Beaumont came out of the ballroom and, spotting them, glided over to join the group. Her gown was a royal blue trimmed with silver thread and seed pearls. Like Kate's it had a high girdle as was the fashion with Venetian ladies of the period, but unlike her sister's gown, which was cut low and off the shoulders, Elizabeth's neckline was squared and enhanced by a Medici collar. She smiled regally when she saw Giles and upon nearing, offered her hand in a way that made her younger sister lift her eyes to the crystal chandelier hanging directly above them.

"Mr. Channing, how delightful to see you again, and what a marvelous costume. Monte Cristo, isn't it?"

"I thought we'd agreed to make it Giles, Elizabeth, and the pleasure's mine." He took her proffered hand and, bowing from the waist, lifted it to his lips. Then he stepped back to admire her costume. "Divine," he murmured gallantly. "No Medici ever looked lovelier."

Teddy thrust out his chest like an indignant rooster. "Isn't anyone going to say something about *my* costume?"

"Yes, darling," Kate chuckled, giving him a quick kiss on his leathery cheek. "Your plume is slipping." She reached up and adjusted the ostrich feather in his hat.

"Oh, Katherine," Elizabeth sighed. "What on earth have you done to your hair?"

"What does it look like? I took out all those awful pins you stuck into it and gave it a good brushing." Kate considered her sister's darker, more golden-blond hair perfectly styled into an intricate chignon and felt an instant of envy. An hour ago her own hair had been tortured into the same look and she'd felt as though she'd been wearing a squirrel's nest on top of her head. Why was it that Elizabeth always managed to appear sophisticated in such styles while she merely looked awkward? "Just who am I supposed to be in this getup anyway?" Kate added, eager to get Elizabeth off the subject of hair.

"Well, Shakespeare's famous Katharina of Padua, of course."

The Shrew. Stiffening, Kate narrowed her eyes at her sister. It wasn't often that Elizabeth indulged in pranks of any sort; older by five years, she'd had to fill their late mother's shoes when she'd barely been more than a girl herself, and she clearly took the role of playing lady of the manor seriously. But once in a while . . .

"Since when is standing up for what you believe in synonymous with being a shrew?" Kate asked with quiet dignity.

"Must you take everything so literally? It was simply too tempting to resist, considering your name *is* Katherine and you do have a tendency to bristle when Dad calls you Wildcat. Anyway, when I saw that gown I knew it was made for you."

"Excuse me, Miss Kate," a servant said, discreetly joining them. "You have a phone call."

Kate thanked him and added that she would take it in her father's study. "If you'll excuse me," she murmured to no one in particular. She eased around her father, never more grateful for an escape in her life.

"When you return, perhaps you'll favor me with a dance, Miss Beaumont?" Giles asked, finding himself reluctant to see her go now that the evening was just beginning to show some promise. How odd—had he just seen a glimmer of hurt in her eyes?

Kate paused only momentarily. The mere thought of being in his arms made her clench her hands into fists. Dance with the man who was going to build Beaumont Center? She would rather eat snails.

"Oh, *do* look for me, Mr. Channing," she purred. And hold your breath while you're at it, she told him with her eyes just before she spun around and walked off.

Ever since grade school, Kate had been aware of the fickleness of life. Back then her best friend had been Missy Wilkes, their gardener's daughter, and they'd attended the same school.

Some of the other children had taken an inordinate pleasure in taunting her and Missy, not so much for their racial differences, but their social ones. Missy would have preferred to retreat and suffer in silence. But even then Kate had been no shrinking violent; she'd opted to confront her schoolmates. Already showing signs of being a tomboy, she'd wrestled a few down to the ground and forced them to apologize.

Not only didn't it stop the taunting, it finally convinced Kate's father to transfer her to a private school where all the girls came from affluent homes like herself. Sadly, that helped end the friendship with Missy. It also made a lasting impression that survived all through Kate's school years and even college.

Now as she stood in the barn, having snuck off to check on her mare, Gypsy, who was due to foal soon, that old despair was resurfacing.

"It's not that I'm not grateful," she explained to the dapple-gray horse, who was more concerned with getting hold of more of the carrot slices Kate had snuck from the buffet tables. "I know that Dad's made some important additions to Atlanta and that if we weren't well off, I would never have been able to have you."

The ration of carrots devoured, the mare made a snorting sound and rubbed her head against her mistress. Kate sighed and gave her the soothing stroking the horse obviously wanted next.

"But this time it's just not fair," Kate continued mournfully. "That complex will swallow an entire city block. Buildings are going to be torn down. No one seems to care if the people who lived there had someplace else to go or not. But I do, and I'm not about to let them be kicked out without a fight." She thought of her phone call earlier. It gave her some comfort to know that a plan was in the works.

Gypsy whinnied and tossed her head. It drew a sympathetic smile from Kate.

"Easy now," she said, stroking her black mane. "You're getting tired of carrying all that extra weight aren't you? Try listening to the music. Hear it?" She tried humming a few bars, but it sounded so bad, she shook her head. "Can you imagine? Here I am, twenty-five-years-old, Dad's invested all that money sending me to those fancy schools, but I still can't carry a note, dance or find the patience to make polite conversation to annoying people. Well, that's okay...I'd rather be out here with you anyway."

Her thoughts drifted to Giles Channing and she unconsciously lifted her chin. He had irked her the most this evening. He was so confident, so polished, so *English*. She only hoped that her father wasn't going to make a habit of bringing him to Meadowbrook. Though she had her own apartment now, she still spent a great deal of time here. The prospect of having to avoid Giles in her own home wasn't one she cared to contemplate. But a moment later she reassured herself.

He was obviously more Elizabeth's type. She was everything Kate never would be: sophisticated, feminine and *finished*, as an instructor in one of her former schools liked to say.

Even now Elizabeth was probably spinning around and around the ballroom in the arms of some dashing looking man, Kate thought as sounds of a waltz drifted over from the house. Elizabeth always did have a talent for attract-

ing gorgeous men. But attract is all it would be, Kate
mused, attempting her best simulation of a waltz. Her sister's greater talent was keeping men at bay. If it hadn't
been for poor Daniel, she doubted Liz would have deigned
to marry anyone.

Funny how in a way they were alike. Kate took a wicked
pleasure in ignoring the line of eligible bachelors her father paraded before her, too. It wasn't because she didn't
think any of them was good enough. She just hated the
way it made her feel—like a prize cow at the state fair. She
didn't have anything against the concept of marriage, in
fact the idea of having a family of her own was one she
often daydreamed about. But she was determined to see
that the man she spent her life with would be one of her
own choosing, not her father's, the paper's society col-
umnist's or anyone else's.

"Not bad, but you're holding your back too stiff."

Kate spun around only to find her worst nightmare realized. Giles Channing stood not more than a few yards
away, casually leaning against the stable wall. His words,
as well as the smile on his face, clearly indicated he'd seen
and heard enough to humiliate her completely. She wanted
nothing less than to sweep up her skirts and run. Instead
she lifted her chin, determined to brazen it out.

"Lost your way to your car, Mr. Channing?"

He tore his gaze from the appealing—too appealing—
picture she made and considered his surroundings. Actually, he *had* been contemplating leaving. Bored, he'd
stepped out to the veranda to indulge in a smoke and consider his options. Then he'd spotted the light on in the
stable. He would have enjoyed a closer examination of
Teddy's stock, but it could wait for another time.

"No," he said, returning his gaze to her. "I found what
I was looking for. You promised me a dance, Katherine."

In the dim light of the single lamp, his striking features were even more classical; his cheekbones were more prominent, his nose sharper, the lines bracketing his firm, chiselled mouth deeper. Kate hated to admit it, but his costume suited him. It emphasized a dash and dignity that seemed intrinsic to the man. She'd never had a problem with holding her own with anyone, but he managed to make her feel naïve and awkward.

"As I'm sure you've already noticed," she began coolly, "it's not one of my favorite activities."

He'd noticed *and* heard. But even if he thought it strange that the privileged daughter of one of the state's wealthiest men couldn't dance, he also knew it clearly wasn't the moment to question her about it.

With a shrug, he moved away from the wall and stepped closer. "Dancing, like riding and making love, is something that requires the right partner to do it well. Would you like me to show you?"

She narrowed her eyes, sure that he was trying to embarrass her. She didn't have much experience in the latter, but he was in for a surprise if he thought she was one of those silly women who behaved as if they were perennial virgins.

"I'm not sure," she murmured, tilting her head to feign consideration. "You see, I don't happen to agree with your comparisons. I ride rather well, myself."

"An experienced woman—my favorite kind."

Heat rose in her cheeks and temper flashed in her eyes. But before she could think of a suitable reply he continued.

"Is this your mount?" He stepped over to Gypsy's stall and stroked the horse's neck with a gentleness that surprised Kate.

"Normally. But as you can see, she's about to foal. Excuse me, I made an assumption. Do *you* ride, Mr. Channing?"

Giles slid his glance from female to female, not at all fooled by the docility in either. "Whenever and wherever I can. It's one of my two greatest passions."

Kate's mouth went dry. Even if it hadn't, she wouldn't have been prepared to answer him. To think that just the other day Elizabeth had mentioned how she much preferred the company of European men over Americans because of the latter's tendency toward brashness. Kate couldn't wait to enlighten her.

To her relief there was an annoyed whinny from the next stall, and then the sound of a hoof kicking into the door. "That's Zulu," she said, relieved to find something else to focus on. She stepped around Giles and went to the next stall where the stallion was tossing his exceptionally long mane and snorting. "I've been riding him since Gypsy's semi-retirement. Now he thinks he owns me."

As she reached into her pocket and gave him the two sugar cubes she'd brought especially for his sweet tooth, Giles eyed the horse with respect. The black stallion was every bit of seventeen hands and there was a glint in his eye that suggested a rider would have to be a fool to take him for granted. But it was also clear, as he watched Zulu lean closer into Kate's tender stroking, that the horse had a weakness for her ministrations.

"He has good taste," Giles drawled. "Interesting name, too."

"It just seemed to fit him. He's fierce and as tireless as a warrior. No one can ride him but me, and even I end up in the dirt occasionally."

"Perhaps you'll allow me to try him sometime?"

She would, if only to have the pleasure of watching him spit dirt and rub his sore backside. Zulu tolerated men least of all. "Perhaps," she murmured.

As she began to turn away, Giles caught her arm. "You're determined not to like me. Why?"

She hadn't expected the direct confrontation, but she respected it enough to give him an honest answer. "You're building my father's project."

"So?"

"I happen to think it's a mistake."

It hardly told him enough, but he would accept that for the moment. "Fine. Then why don't we simply avoid the subject. Instead I'll tell you about myself— I'm really a nice fellow once you get to know me."

She wouldn't be charmed. With an agitated look, she tried to free her arm.

Giles secured his hold by grasping her wrist. "Listen." Strains from another tune drifted through the opened stable doors. "Chopin. Who can resist dancing to one of his waltzes?"

"Me," Kate replied as Giles tried to draw her toward him. She held back. "I told you, I don't like to dance. More important, I don't *want* to."

"Katherine, there's nothing to be afraid of."

"I'm not afraid—and don't call me Katherine."

"Why not?" He closed one hand around hers and slipped his other hand around her waist. "Katherine . . . it's a lovely, feminine name. It suits you."

"About as much as ribbons and lace do."

"You think not? I don't know. The wonderful thing about women is that they're as versatile as they are unpredictable. That's what makes them such an irresistible mystery to men."

"You needn't waste your energy trying to flatter me, Mr. Channing, I'm not interested."

"Correction—you don't want to be. In fact, you're condemning me without even giving me the opportunity to defend myself. I'm deeply wounded, Kate. By the way, don't look now, but you're doing rather well."

She glanced down. Just as she realized they were indeed dancing, she stumbled.

"I said, don't look. Listen to the music and follow my lead."

"I—I can't hear it well enough." Not with the pounding of her heartbeat suddenly echoing like kettle drums in her ears. She tried to pull away, but he didn't let her.

"I'll hum it for you," he said, giving her a lazy smile.

His voice was a rich tenor, his pitch as perfect as hers was awful. It was only another reason for her to decide she couldn't stand him. "This is really ridiculous," she insisted, becoming increasingly embarrassed.

He slipped his hand lower to the base of her spine. "Just watch me and not our feet and follow the pressure of my hand."

But she couldn't look at him when they were this close. It made the pounding in her ears even worse. She settled for fixing her gaze on his cravat and wondering how many droplets of moisture would have to slide down her back before he felt them permeate her gown.

Giles was too busy concentrating on her face to notice anything else. She was truly lovely, disturbingly so. Her face was oval, her features delicate. Forehead, cheekbones, nose, all were as fine as if molded from porcelain, and almost as translucent. Even that mouth, which seemed predisposed to fling barbs at him, was exquisitely shaped and tempting. Asleep, she would look like an angel with her ash-blond hair spread like luxurious silk over a pillow. Awake...Teddy was right in calling her Wildcat. She would be a handful for any man.

Giles preferred tranquility to pugnaciousness, and yet there was something about her that drew him. Could it be that what he recognized was valiancy rather than rebelliousness? He wasn't quite certain; but there was something about the way she lifted her chin, something in the directness of her gaze that didn't allow him to dismiss her as a petulant heiress.

Perhaps it would help to learn more about why she was against her father's project—though there was damned little she could do to stop it. The sooner she accepted that, the easier it would be on everyone. At any rate, he'd been on target about one thing: in the right hands—namely his—she *could* dance.

How easy he made it seem, she thought. How fluid their movements were as he spun her around and around. For a few moments incredulous delight replaced disbelief and she glanced up at him, only to see his sculpted mouth curled in a sardonic smile.

The spell was instantly shattered. She stopped.

"Thank you. You've made your point."

"Kate, admit it, you were enjoying yourself."

"I said thank you."

As she began to pull away, he tightened his hold. "But not politely at all, my dear. Perhaps I should collect a fee to assuage my hurt feelings." Without giving her time to question or protest, he drew her back into his arms and closed his mouth over hers.

Kate clenched her fingers into fists, clearly intending to deliver her own surprise; but before intention could be galvanized into action, his warmth and strength seeped into her, flooding her senses and drowning the impulse. Stunned, she opened her eyes only to find him watching her, and what she saw in their depths made her legs nearly buckle beneath her.

Desire—it had never come to him more quickly. Like a punch to the head, he was dizzy with it. What had begun as a mercurial whim was suddenly a need and, giving into it, he raised his hand to her cheek to ask for more.

For a moment she lost all sense of herself, all rational thought but to feel, and she parted her lips to his full exploration. He was gentle, yet thorough. He used patience and generosity to fan the heat rising within her, and when he coaxed her into matching the seductive rhythm of his tongue, she obeyed because she didn't want the delicious sensations it elicited to stop.

It was the sound of her name on his lips, a name she'd never felt comfortable with, said in a way she'd never heard it whispered, that brought back a corner of sanity. She pushed herself away from him, even though her legs felt too weak to bear her weight. She only knew she had to move, she had to get away.

Without a word, she ran out of the stables and disappeared into the darkness.

Two

___

"Good morning, all." Showing none of the trepidation she felt, Kate breezed into the formal dining room the next morning. Circling around Elizabeth, she paused at the head of the table where her father sat in a carved armchair and gave him a kiss on the cheek.

Teddy glanced up from his morning paper, awarding her a mock look of confusion over the rims of his reading glasses. "Do I know you? I was expecting my daughter—the one who disappeared from my party last night without even saying good-night."

"Sorry." She glanced over at her sister, receiving a look that clearly asked, *what did you expect?*, and dropped her gaze to the 18th-century Aubusson carpet patterned in shades of rose and cream. Her rehearsed explanation was a cliché, but still preferable to telling the truth. "I developed this splitting headache and I went upstairs to lie down."

Teddy frowned, his stark eyebrows drawing into one intimidating line. But there was concern rather than disbelief in his blue-gray eyes and a rough gentleness in the grasp of the large hand that covered hers as she rested it on his shoulder. "You don't say? But, sweetheart, you never get headaches. Are you feeling all right now? Maybe you should call the doctor."

"It's gone," Kate insisted, eager to put the deception behind her. But another glance toward Elizabeth, pursing her lips as she spooned up a portion of pink grapefruit from her fruit cup, spawned an irresistible impulse. "I guess that hairdo Liz originally tried on me was even more irritating to my scalp than anyone could have guessed."

"My, our creativity is really working overtime this morning," Elizabeth drawled, touching her napkin to her lips. Spreading it back on her lap, she gave her sister a dry smile. "Don't worry, Dad, she didn't miss the entire ball. Wasn't it around nine that I saw you running up from the stables, Kate?"

Kate barely suppressed a groan. Elizabeth might look fresh and serene this morning in her white linen suit, with her hair smoothed into its normal chin-length style; but beneath that guileless facade was a shrewd woman with the instincts of a bloodhound. The question was, how much more had she seen?

"I had to check on Gypsy," she replied with a careless shrug. She wandered over to the buffet and lifted the silver cover off one dish to inspect its contents. "I thought the fresh air might do my headache some good."

"That's certainly what I would have done. I wonder if Giles Channing was having the same problem? I saw him coming up from that direction a few minutes later."

Game, set, match . . . Kate wrinkled her nose, but not at the poached eggs she was inspecting. "If you say so," she said, replacing the lid with vigor and reaching for the next one.

"Considering all the time you spend driving back and forth because of that horse, I think you should move back here until she foals," Teddy grumbled, reaching for the fragile Limoges coffee cup that all but disappeared in his beefy hand.

"*You* think I should never have moved out," Kate amended dryly, though she could have hugged him for choosing this moment to lobby for her return. She would welcome almost any conversation as long as it kept Elizabeth from any further mention of her disappearance last night or Giles Channing. Heaven knew she had enough on her mind without dealing with that.

"Well, why not when we have this big house and a chauffeur who could easily drive you to that job of yours?"

She really did miss sleeping in her old bedroom, as she had last night. She missed being with her family—despite her father's coddling and her sister's lectures. But her need and determination to establish her independence were stronger.

"Dad, Clarence has a tendency to ignore traffic lights and stop signs in that part of town. Besides, people might think it's inappropriate for one of the directors of ABA to be seen arriving at work in a chauffeured limousine. After all, A Better Atlanta's urban development projects are funded by private donations and we operate on a no-frills budget."

Teddy's answer to that was a bearlike growl, and he set the cup back onto its delicate saucer with a force that made Elizabeth wince. "Excuse me, what do I know? I'm just a father who's spent a small fortune putting his child through top-notch schools so that she could end up having to live off her trust fund because her employer can't afford to pay her."

"They can afford to pay me, Daddy. I just don't take the money."

That only upset him more. He yanked off his glasses, his expression changing to one of disbelief. "Girl, I think you need to go back to school and take a few more business classes. The whole point of working and being in business is to make money."

"I know that, and the center did make a handsome profit last quarter...so we're going to buy a lot near one of those low-rent housing projects and put in a park for the kids. Morning, Leona," she said to their housekeeper, who came through the swinging doors carrying a fresh pot of coffee. "Are all the waffles gone?"

The moon-faced woman gave her an amused grin. "Gone where, child? You know your daddy gots to have his poached eggs and ham, and Miss Chicken Bones over there is living on air and fruit. Check the last dish. The sausages are in there with them. I'll bring out the syrup I got warming for you just as soon as I refill everyone's coffee."

Kate loaded her plate before taking her seat across from Elizabeth, who looked from the waffles to her own fruit cup and sighed. "Want some?" Kate offered, her smile mischievous because Leona was listening and required little more to get her started.

"Very funny," Elizabeth mumbled.

"It wouldn't hurt you to eat something substantial for a change," Leona said, right on cue. "That wouldn't keep a dog's tail wagging for five minutes. Let me fix you a spoonful of scrambled eggs and a slice of toast."

After shooting her sister a speaking glance, Elizabeth politely declined. "I have a Junior League luncheon today."

"So what's that but a bunch of heifers munching on ruffage?"

Kate hid her smile behind her coffee cup. "She read an article the other day that said by the time a woman reaches thirty she's put on an average of twenty-three pounds. She's determined to be an exception to the rule."

"Elizabeth Beaumont Kirkland, have you lost all your good sense? Child, you and your sister got the two smallest waists in Cobb County, and *you're* two inches taller!" Throwing up her hand and declaring to Providence that she didn't know what this younger generation had come to, Leona withdrew to the kitchen.

"Thank you so much, Katherine," Elizabeth intoned. "I just love to be lectured to as if I were twelve years old again."

"Now you know how I feel whenever you lay into me."

"I do not *lay* into you. I merely voice my concern over the image you present. For instance your attire this morning. I thought you said you were going to have to go to work? What kind of businesswoman goes anywhere dressed like that?" she asked, inclining her head at Kate's white shirt and jeans.

"We aren't all born to be clotheshorses." Kate picked up a sausage link with her fingers and took a bite.

"But do we have to run around looking like stablehands?"

"Since when can stablehands afford Calvin Klein's?"

"You two stop cackling like a couple of hens and let your daddy read," Leona scolded, returning with Kate's warm maple syrup. She poured a generous portion over the waffles and set the pitcher on the table before heading back into the kitchen.

But Teddy was through with his reading and put away his paper. "Kate, if you're going to be here after all, why don't you come over and join us at the demolition site? We'll take Channing for lunch afterward."

Elizabeth shook her head in disbelief. "You know how she feels about Beaumont Center, Dad. And if last night was any indication, she's not much fonder of Giles Channing."

Kate thought of the man whose jade-green eyes had haunted her in her sleep, and she poked her fork rather brutally into a piece of waffle. "I'm sorry, Dad, but she's right. Anyway, my day's full. Rusty Maxwell and I—uh—have to inspect some lots for the park."

"I'm sorry, too." For a moment Teddy watched his younger daughter attack her breakfast, until another troubled frown furrowed his brow. "You know, kitten, I respect your right to disagree about my business decisions, but you know how I feel about making a guest feel welcome."

"I don't think you have to worry about Mr. Channing," Kate replied, wishing the man would catch the next flight out of Atlanta and never come back. "He strikes me as someone who makes himself at home wherever he goes."

Unbidden, the memory of his kiss came back again; the way their lips had seemed to fit so well, the way the kiss had gone from impulsive to ardent.... She gave herself a mental shake and reached for her napkin, this time rubbing it firmly against her lips.

"At any rate," she added, "it's not as though he'll be around for long, right? I would think he's the chain-of-command type. Comes in, signs the contract, then leaves the dirty work to the architects, engineers and what have you until it's time to celebrate the grand opening and take a bow.''

''No, he's a hands-on person. Oh, Orion Development remains based out of Miami and he'll be in and out of there or checking on one of their other projects, but he's going to be here as much as possible until the center is completed. Why I even tried to get him to take a room right here at Meadowbrook, seeing how we'll be working so closely together. But he insisted it would be better if he looked for an apartment closer to the job site.''

''Thank God for small favors,'' Kate muttered into her coffee.

''Of course, we do plan to have him over for dinner as often as we can,'' Elizabeth added with a bit more relish than Kate thought necessary. ''He also enjoys riding—did he happen to mention that to you? No, that's right, you barely spoke. Well, Dad said he should talk to you about finding a suitable mount.''

Her appetite destroyed, Kate shoved her plate away. ''Why aren't *you* going with Dad this morning?'' she asked with saccharine sweetness, her frustration beginning to get the best of her. ''You might not be able to stay for lunch, but surely there'll be a ceremonial ribbon to cut or something. I haven't seen your picture on the society pages of the paper for weeks now.''

''Just because you're feeling edgy—'' Seeing the flash of regret in her sister's eyes, Elizabeth sighed. ''Forget it. Anyway, I can't go, either. I promised Susan Murdock that I'd help her choose wallpaper and carpeting for her new house. Her appointment with the decorator's at ten.''

Teddy pushed himself to his feet. ''Well, since you're both determined to make me go by myself, I might as well leave. Have a good day,'' he said, moving around the table to give them each a kiss. "Remind Leona not to hold supper for me. I'm having a dinner meeting in town."

He was barely out the door when Elizabeth also stood. For a moment Katherine studied her sister, taking in the perfectly coiffed golden hair, the gleaming pearls at her throat and her graceful, manicured hands. Kate was secretly in near awe of her sister, believing she was the most gorgeous woman she'd ever seen; but sometimes Kate wished Elizabeth was a little less . . . perfect.

"I'm sorry for being a witch," she said on impulse.

Halfway to the door, Elizabeth hesitated before stepping back to the table. "Do you want to talk?"

She wished they could. But Elizabeth wouldn't understand. More than likely she would throw a fit. Kate wasn't sure she even understood this tension churning in her herself. She'd thought it was because of the project and her plans, but now . . .

"Kate, you're not going to do anything foolish are you?"

Foolish? Kate stiffened. "I don't think I deserve that. Just because I stand up for what I believe in—"

"Stand up for what you believe in? Is that what you were doing when you took the dean of your college hostage?"

"What we did was stage a sit-in at the administration building to protest the biased hiring against women faculty members. Dean Hanover was the only one who thought he was being taken hostage. Anyway, that's ancient history."

"You always have a reasonable explanation for everything. What about last year's little fiasco when the governor was visiting during his re-election campaign? Dad was part of the VIP group taking a tour of the new bottling plant, but the media was focused on you in a picket line protesting the postponement of that water treatment project. You don't seem to realize that as a Beaumont everything you do gets put under a microscope and magnified.''

"And that's bad?"

With a helpless shake of her head, Elizabeth circled the rest of the way around the table to stroke her sister's long, silky hair. "I don't know, Kate. I only know it's awkward for me to be put in a position of explaining why you do what you do at every social function I have to attend. That might sound priggish to you, but I'm simply not the rebel you are."

As far as confessions went, that was a blockbuster. Kate tilted her head to touch her cheek to Elizabeth's hand that came to rest on Kate's shoulder. "I'm sorry you're going to be on your own for dinner this evening," she told her, aware that Elizabeth had moved back into their father's house after Daniel's death to avoid being alone.

"Why don't you join me. You'll be by to check on Gypsy anyway," Elizabeth teased. "Tell you what, I'll pick up some Chinese take-out on my way home and we'll give Leona the night off. We can eat out on the porch the way we did when we were kids and I made peanut butter and honey on crackers."

They would invariably talk about Mother and Kate would always end up crying. Back then it seemed the hurt was never going to go away. "They're calling for rain," she murmured, even now feeling a lump in her throat.

"You like the rain. Anyway, the porch is covered."

But evening was still hours away and a lot could happen between now and then. Enough to make Elizabeth forget this whimsical exchange. By then she might not only have decided to cancel their plans, she might wish she could deny they were even related. Still, a person had to follow her own heart and her own sense of values....

"Okay, it's a deal," Kate said, optimistic enough to hope it might all work out. "Have a good day."

Elizabeth hesitated a second before giving her sister's hair a gentle tug. "You too, baby. At least try to stay out of trouble."

As Elizabeth left the dining room, Kate checked her watch and deciding to snatch up another link of sausage after all, stood. It was getting late and she needed to get moving, too.

"Sorry, Liz," she murmured under her breath. "Getting into trouble, is all but inevitable. The challenge is going to be to stay out of jail."

"I don't know what it is, but this project has me feeling like a youngster starting out fresh again," Teddy said as Clarence drove the limousine into the area designated for VIPs and the press.

Beside him, Giles smiled and nodded. He was aware of a knot of tension or excitement twisting in his own belly; however, in his case, he wasn't sure if it was a result of the job or something far more complex.

"You have a right to be excited *and* proud. It's not every day a person begins a project that will bear his name for generations to come," he replied with ingrained politeness. "At any rate, I think you show a zestful approach to everything you do. That is if last night's celebration was anything to go by."

"You had a good time then? I'm glad. This morning I found out that my Kate developed a headache and went to her room."

"I'm sorry to hear that." Giles had to work at keeping his lips from twitching. A headache, was it? Well, he'd developed a certain side effect, as well, but it hadn't been any headache. "I hope she's feeling better this morning?"

"Fit as a fiddle. You can't keep Kate Beaumont down for long. She takes after her old man in that respect."

The vehicle came to a halt and the two men stepped out. They were immediately met by someone handing them yellow hard hats. Teddy's assistant came over, clipboard in hand, and informed him that the mayor and his entourage were on their way.

"Wonderful," Teddy replied, waving to the chief of the fire department who was being briefed by his own people. The police were in place, too, patrolling the barricaded streets to keep out vehicles as well as pedestrian traffic. The sun was bright and the breeze minimal. Teddy gripped the lapels of his suit jacket and grinned. "Keep it running smooth, boys. No glitches."

Giles shook hands with Steve Nolan, the architect, who'd joined them. Steve showed him a map passed on from the head of the wrecking crew indicating where the charges would be placed throughout the buildings that, when set off, would create one great implosion. The buildings weren't overly high. That and the fact that they were far enough away from the center of town so as not to seriously impede normal activity in the city, was the only reason approval to do the leveling on a weekday during regular business hours was granted.

"Can't you just see it?" Teddy mused, gazing up at the old building that would soon become a heap of rubble. "Beaumont Center is going to rejuvenate this part of the neighborhood. It's going to be a jewel sparkling in the sun. At night the glass-domed theater will glow like a pearl. Neighborhood kids will come to throw pennies in the fountains—"

"More likely pick them out," someone behind Giles amended dryly.

There was a round of laughter, except from Teddy, who told his assistant to make a note to look into outdoor security guards as well as the guards for inside. Someone else edged through the growing crowd, bringing a list that forced Giles to concentrate on the immediate.

The sun was already hot and the humidity was intensifying. If they didn't get their TV interviews over with soon, they were going to melt in their business suits. It didn't look good for VIPs to be seen sweating on TV, no matter what the reason.

Giles passed on the message to Teddy and the two excused themselves and began to walk toward the press stations. Someone else shoved his way toward them and asked them to wait. It was the head of the demolition team.

"We have a glitch," he said, removing his own hard hat to wipe away sweat and dust from his forehead.

"No glitches," Teddy replied firmly.

"There's a protest group."

"Get the police to keep them outside the barricades."

"They're inside one of the buildings."

"*What?* How did they manage that?" Teddy demanded, and just as abruptly waved away the question. "Never mind. Get the police and get them out. *Carry* them if you have to."

"The press," Teddy's assistant warned him under his breath.

"They've shackled themselves to structural beams," the demolitions man said with equal urgency. "And one of them says she's your daughter."

"My *what*?" Teddy's face screwed up as though he'd just swallowed the most bitter of pills.

Beside him, Giles did his best not to laugh. So the delectable Miss Beaumont was more than simply temper and accusation.

"What are you going to do?" he asked her father.

The older man looked down at his hands, clenched as though in a stranglehold. "I've never laid a hand on that girl in her life," he murmured half to himself. "Even when she was nine and snuck into that truck delivering feed and drove it through the back of the barn." Slowly, he lifted his gaze to his assistant. "Find me a convent...with walls. Big walls."

Giles chuckled and laid a calming hand on Teddy's shoulder. "Hold on a moment. Maybe we can work something out. Has she or anyone else made any demands?" he asked the demolitions man.

"They're waiting to talk to someone with authority."

"I'll give her authority," Teddy vowed, taking a step toward the street.

Giles tightened his hold. "Wait. Let me go. You're too emotionally involved," he explained when Teddy began to protest.

It took a bit more persuading, but finally the older man conceded. "All right. Maybe it's best that you try to reason with her first it'll give me a chance to calm down. But you tell her—all of them—that those buildings are coming down."

Giles slid out of his pearl-gray suit jacket and matching vest, handing both to his assistant. Then he stripped off his tie and loosened the top two buttons of his white shirt.

"What the devil are you doing that for?" Teddy demanded.

"To gain an edge," Giles replied with a crooked smile. "It won't help to look like the establishment. Why don't you figure out a way to keep the press from getting too suspicious." With a nod to the demolitions man, they headed for the street.

Like most cities, Atlanta had its polished side where commerce thrived and tourists gathered. There buildings looked like runway models, tall and sleek, often breathtaking. Scattered between them flowerbeds rose from concrete, tended by unseen hands and always immaculate. It was the side of the city that everyone liked to focus on.

But also like most cities, Atlanta had a less photogenic side. Here the city suffered from neglect, even abuse. Whatever beauty these buildings once possessed, it had worn away long ago, worn to the point that a vivid imagination wasn't enough to visualize what had been. However, change was coming here, as well. The stretching finger of progress was within minutes of making its initial mark.

And not a moment too soon, Giles thought as he followed the demolitions man down an alley to a side entrance. The scent of decay was rank and seemed to close in on him. It made him think of a line from a favorite poem, about one age dying only to give birth to another. This place was dying, but what would be built from the rubble would bring new life.

"I'll go in alone," he said when they reached the doorway.

The man who'd introduced himself as Detweiler hesitated, then gave him a rueful smile. "Suit yourself. This was the last checkpoint. If you can get them out, we'll be ready to count down in about fifteen minutes."

Giles understood the underlying message; it was the same one that would influence any project like this. *Time is money.* "I'll do what I can," he replied.

Once he stepped inside the dark room, he paused to allow his vision to adjust. He heard a murmur of voices and a gasp. He didn't like being at a disadvantage, but it lasted only seconds.

Soon he was able to ascertain that the room was huge and empty except for the half dozen people either tied or chained to the steel support beams that lined the length of it. He glanced at each person in succession. The feeble ones looked nervous but still as committed as their younger companions. Giles had to admire their courage. Then his gaze rested on Kate.

Sitting on the dusty cement floor, her hands locked behind her, she looked smaller than he'd remembered, but no less attractive. As he eyed the lavender bandanna tying back her hair, the white short-sleeved shirt, jeans and high-topped sneakers, it finally struck him why Detweiler wanted to accompany him. He couldn't blame the man. She was easy to look at. She was also hot, but clearly no less determined than the others. Not very happy to see him, either, he noted, deciding the gasp he'd heard had come from her. He, ironically enough, was taking an inordinate pleasure in having her as a captive audience.

He crossed over to her and crouched down. "We meet again, fair Kate."

Her answering look should have given him second-degree burns. "What are you doing here?" she demanded stiffly.

"Why, you asked for someone in authority, didn't you?" He quickly lifted a finger to caution her as she began to reply. "I don't think you really want to talk to Teddy right now. His coloring has improved, but he was muttering something about convents with moats when I left him."

That had her drawing her lower lip between her teeth. Giles recalled how sweet those lips had tasted and how malleable they'd been beneath the firm pressure of his.

It had been sheer impulse to kiss her and, just like in the old days when his beloved but sober-minded nanny used to predict leisurely repentance being the heir of hasty decisions, he'd lain awake for hours searching for an ounce of wisdom in his actions.

He adored women, as friends, as business associates...and admittedly he'd indulged in his share of liaisons. Was he a flirt? Unapologetically. But despite the stories of broken engagements that were occasionally printed, he'd never, not even temporarily, lost his head over one.

This woman could change that. This woman could become a preoccupation. The realization was both appealing and unsettling. As tempting as she was, he reminded himself, she was also trouble, and the timing couldn't be worse for either malady.

"Well, I'm sorry Daddy's upset, but it can't be helped," she told him, her mind made up. "Our demands have to be heard."

"All right. Have your say and we'll get you cut loose."

Kate compressed her lips in an attempt to temper her annoyance. "Don't patronize me, Mr. Channing. What you can do is write them down and have my father add his signature attesting to his intention to meet those demands."

"The only thing your father might agree to at this point is not having your pretty scalp, my dear. And why on earth haven't you approached him on a civil level before?"

"Don't you think I've tried?" She leaned her head back against the steel beam and closed her eyes. "He groups my work with Elizabeth's annual charity bazaar. He tells me not to trouble myself with *unpleasant* things, that that's why he's worked so hard to be a success, so we can enjoy the good life.

"But there's a great injustice being done here," she added, lowering her voice to an urgent whisper because she could see the others were eyeing her worriedly. "Do you know what this room used to be? A church for the homeless and the abused. That's Reverend Mitchell at the last pole. Beside him is Gus Huett and his sister Franny. They survive solely on social security and were renting one of the apartments above, until they received their eviction notice. They've tried to find alternate housing close to the city hospital, because Franny needs constant medical supervision, but it's been impossible. Thanks to all this renovating, the nearest thing they can afford is out beyond where the bus lines run, and neither of them drives."

Giles shifted to glance over to the elderly couple, only to find that everyone was watching *him* and in a way that made him feel like the villain in an old silent movie who rightly deserved his comeuppance. "I assure you that I had no idea about any of this. It's not my habit to put anyone into the streets."

As he stood up, she stared, unsure of what any of that meant. "Where are you going?"

"To get you results. I'll be back in five minutes."

He was back in three. With him was her father, who might not have seemed near a stroke, but neither did he look forgiving.

"Well, young lady," Teddy said, scowling at her companions before resting his gaze on her. "It appears you've been doing some fast talking to Channing here."

"I'd have talked to you, Daddy, if you'd only have listened."

Teddy scratched the back of his neck and shot Giles a side-long look. "Damn it all—I thought we've been through all this before? You know I have nothing but good intentions for this city. Can't you see that a hotel will bring added revenue to the community, not to mention create an opportunity for new jobs? There'll be shops and restaurants, too. And what about the theater and galleries? I'm bringing culture to the people!"

"To *some* people, Daddy. I don't argue that your center isn't a beautiful idea; but beauty tarnishes when it demands a moral price. I know these are only a few people, but are we supposed to sacrifice the minority to benefit the majority?"

"What about the benefits of cleaning up the city and creating a cultural environment?"

"What good is culture if you can't afford the price of the ticket to see it?" she shot back. Sighing, she bowed her head. "Sometimes I'm so ashamed of us. We think more and bigger is better, and when we see someone in the streets who couldn't keep up, who's dirty and homeless, we get annoyed at them for visually offending us. The least they could do is buy a bar of soap from the money they panhandle, right?"

Giles stared at Kate as if seeing her for the first time. Maybe he was, he decided. He'd thought her spoiled, yet her conscience ran very near the surface. He'd thought her temperamental, yet what had she said that wasn't sound? He'd listened to her talk about justice last night and classified her as simply another person whose heart was in the right place, but, like the majority, appeased her conscience by writing a check once a year to a charity only to have the bulk of the donation spent on administrative expenses.

She was doing something about her disquiet. It was a helluva lot more than they could say for themselves.

Giles glanced at Teddy and saw that he, too, was deep in thought. What he didn't expect was for the businessman to reach into his suit jacket, draw out a handkerchief and wipe his eyes.

"What do you say?" he asked the older man.

"I say it's a fine day that a man has to learn a lesson in ethics from the runt of his litter," he grumbled before shooting Giles a wry but proud smile. "She's a pistol, my Kate." As his eyes filled again, he gestured awkwardly and he turned away. "Well, don't just stand there, Channing, find out what these people need. I have to—I have to go calm down the mayor. The man's always in such a damned hurry."

As Teddy shuffled out, Giles crouched back down before Kate and smiled at her wide-eyed stare. "Surprised?"

"This is the first time he's—" She shook her head, feeling a burning behind her own eyes. Turning her attention to the notebook Giles drew from his pocket, she took a deep breath. They'd won, but there was no time to reflect on it or celebrate.

"Go on," he prompted softly.

She was so thirsty, she had to lick her lips. "A building." She cleared her throat. "We need a building comparable in size to this, to be renovated into low-cost housing for the people displaced by this project. In addition to that, there should be another building, either attached or nearby to be used as a church and crisis center by Reverend Mitchell."

Giles listened and wrote. It took him three pages from his note pad before she finished, but even quick calculations told him that she wasn't asking for anything extraordinary.

"And we don't want a free ride," she said in conclusion. "Rent will be paid comparable to what was paid here."

"Fair enough," Giles replied, closing the pad.

Kate studied him more intently, curious and not a little suspicious. "Why?" she asked finally.

He didn't pretend not to understand. "I happen to think you're right," he said shrugging. "I'll go have Teddy sign these and send in someone to cut you loose. Before I do there *is* one more stipulation. I want you to agree to have dinner with me."

Kate felt her spirits plunge along with her heart. "I'd rather be exiled to that convent and dig the moat myself."

"Be careful of what you wish for, my dear. Of course, if you really *were* only paying lip service with your concern for these gentle souls . . ." He began to rise.

"Wait!" She watched him crouch back down and, when triumph flashed in his pale green eyes, she felt heat scorch her cheeks. *"Why?"* she whispered again, dropping her gaze to the opened collar of his shirt. It wasn't much safer; she became too aware of the attractive contrast of his tanned skin against his white shirt and the hint of crisp black hair matting his chest.

He waited until she lifted her gaze to meet his. "Let's just say that it will even things out a bit. This way we'll all end up paying something."

"What are *you* paying?" she scoffed.

"Why the dinner tab, of course."

She shot him a seething look. "Be serious. You don't really approve of me. I can't believe you'd want to have dinner with me just to make me uncomfortable."

He lifted an eyebrow and let his gaze wander once more to her lips. The hunger to taste her again came swiftly. "I don't know. How uncomfortable could I make you, sweet Kate?"

As she realized the answer to that, the heat in her cheeks spread. It swept through her blood like wildfire, making her aware of herself in a wholly physical way. Sorely tempted to lash out and kick him in the shins, she settled for a venomous glare. "I want your word that you won't try to kiss me again," she demanded in a voice that shook with pent-up emotion.

He pretended to give it serious consideration and finally expelled a deep sigh. "All right. But you're going to have to promise that if I happen to slip up, you won't kiss me back as you did last night. After all, I'm only human."

"You—you *swine*!"

Chuckling, Giles ran his finger down the length of her pert nose and stood. With a roguish tip of his hard hat, he left her to locate Teddy.

"You know the more I think about this agreement I've made, the more I see the genius in it," Teddy said as he and Giles entered his office hours later. "Everyone's happy and I've acquired a tax write-off I hadn't thought of before."

Not *everyone*, Giles mused, his thoughts on Kate. He smiled to himself as he remembered the look she'd given him when she and her friends exited the building. He'd half expected a bolt of lightning to spilt the concrete beneath his feet.

Teddy saw the smile and rubbed at his jaw. "I owe you for handling this so smoothly. I've never met anyone who's dealt with Kate more successfully." His expression grew sly. "You know, I think I may be targeting you for the wrong daughter."

Having just poured himself a glass of ice water from the crystal decanter on a sidebar, Giles paused in reaching for the glass. "I beg your pardon?"

"I'm getting old, Channing," Teddy declared, sitting down in the soft leather chair behind his desk. "I want to bounce some grandkids on my knees before arthritis sets in. But I can't see Elizabeth accommodating me anytime in the foreseeable future, and—well, you've had a sampling of Kate in action and survived the experience better than most."

Good grief, Giles thought, the man was *serious*. He lifted his glass and drank the ice water, buying himself time to think.

All right, so perhaps he was attracted to the minx, and perhaps the thought of settling down had run through his mind a time or two since seeing the effect marriage had had on O'Keefe. But when he chose his life's partner—and that was a contingent *when*—he wanted her to be someone who he could communicate with reasonably, intelligently. Not someone with whom verbal warfare became a replacement for foreplay.

"I would sweeten the deal," Teddy coaxed, interpreting Giles's silence as consideration. "Tell you what...you marry Kate and as a wedding present, I'll sign over half interest in Beaumont Center to you."

Giles returned the glass to the tray and, with a rueful shake of his head, crossed the room to take a seat facing the older man. "It's a tempting offer, but I'm afraid I'm going to have to decline. The Channing family Bible lists more than its share of arranged marriages and, while I have to admit some were quite successful unions, I've always asserted that when it came time for *me* to wed—and mind you wedlock isn't immediate on my list of objectives—it would be for love and nothing less."

Teddy twisted his face into a disgruntled frown. "Wish I could argue with that, but I can't. When I married my Ginnie, I knew she deserved better. Still I was determined to put my ring on her finger." He drummed his stubby fingers on his desk blotter. "All right. I won't mention it again—but the offer stands. Hell, take any daughter. You have my blessings."

Giles rubbed the back of his neck, helpless to stop a low laugh. "You're a man of incredible wit, Teddy."

"Hmph. What I am is desperate."

Three

It was a week before Giles called her. The delay wasn't intentional; he simply got busy and had to put it off.

The wrecking crew hadn't even finished excavation and already his engineers were hounding him about schedules and modifications. The chamber of commerce had consigned him as a one-man advertising campaign for the city. This person had a question, that group had a complaint, and he'd spent yesterday at the main office in Miami. There was no way around it; his personal life had to be put on hold.

Under normal circumstances, he wouldn't have minded. He loved his job and excelled at administrating. It gave him great satisfaction to be able to take an idea and make it work; put this group to this task, ease the tension born of that proposal with another more agreeable, and so on.

But he knew Kate wouldn't buy any of it. He knew she was probably taking his silence in the worst possible way, a device to keep her dangling…he could only imagine. He could even picture her fury and, despite everything, it made him grin. His guess was that she was the type who preferred to get unpleasantness over with, like the child who gulped down vegetables so as to be free to linger over a favorite portion of dinner. Only he wasn't sure he would care to be delegated to the same category as an unwanted vegetable.

Still, it wasn't his intention to be unkind. He wanted her to like him, and he had every intention of providing an enjoyable dinner. Somewhere exemplary but subdued, so as not to make her impatient to have the obligation behind her. With the aid of good wine and a pleasant, private environment, they would talk, get to know each other. He would make her see that he really admired her for what she'd done, and she would come to know that he was more than the reported magnate and playboy. They would become friends. It was all nicely planned in his mind. But his plans were going awry.

When he finally had things back on track, he phoned her. He phoned her at Meadowbrook, and the housekeeper gave him Kate's office number. He called there but she was never in. It took a bit of coaxing but he got her apartment number.

For two days he left messages—on her answering machine, at her office, with the housekeeper. She didn't return any of them, and he came to the conclusion that there was a great deal of truth to the adage about there being nothing quite like a woman who thinks she's being scorned.

With that in mind, he knew he had a decision to make. He could forget the whole thing—and wouldn't that be a relief to her?—or do something. But what was a man to do when faced with the unconventional?

He could simply accept defeat; however, he quickly decided to reject that idea. It went against the grain. There had been Channings at Waterloo and with Gordon at Khartoum. Besides, they had a deal. It was a matter of honor, and one way or another he was going to see she lived up to her part of it.

Looking at it from that perspective gave him an idea, and on the morning of the third day he made a different sort of phone call. Only time would tell him if Kate Beaumont was enough of a traditionalist to appreciate it.

"Kate, you know I'm thrilled that you've got Reverend Mitchell and the others their building," Rusty Maxwell began as he slumped back in his threadbare executive chair, his feet resting on the edge of his desk. He pointed what was left of his bologna-and-cheese sandwich at her. "And you know under normal circumstances, I would be tickled that you talked Big Daddy into letting ABA oversee the renovations. But, kiddo, you've seen our project schedules. Our crews are booked solid for the rest of the summer."

On the other side of the desk, Kate picked up her bag of potato chips, peered inside and found one more chip. She popped it into her mouth and calmly eyed the head of their organization. "When have we ever turned anyone away who needed help?"

"But we're all putting in ten to twelve hour days as it is."

Kate crumpled the empty bag and, gauging the distance to Rusty's wastebasket, tossed it in a high arc for an impressive rim shot. "I'll supervise the renovations and do my regular work on my free time," she said matter-of-factly.

That nearly had the strapping man choking on his lunch. He sat up and hit his chest with his fist. "Kate, you're the best strategist on the team, the biggest fundraiser, the most tireless worker—but you don't know squat about overseeing a renovation project.''

"So I'll learn, and what I don't know, you can teach me. You could also give me Gorman and Martinez. They're almost finished with that resale shop on Delaney Street. I'll manage.''

"I was going to put them on the park detail.''

"Waste of talent, and I'll need a good carpenter and electrician. Tell you what, let me supervise *and* have Gorman and Martinez, and not only will I find you a donor for the park's swings and stuff, I'll get it landscaped. Ted Vandergriff at Piedmont Nurseries is a golf buddy of Daddy's.''

Groaning, Rusty popped the rest of his sandwich into his mouth. "Will you stop tempting me. Anyway, the work's too tough for you. Look at your hands and those puny arms. You wouldn't last more than a few hours swinging a hammer.''

Kate stopped midway in lifting her can of soda to her lips, her expression indignant. "I've done just about everything else there was to do. Come on, Rusty. Part of the reason my father assigned us this project was because I told him I'd run it. Think of the publicity this will bring us.''

The senior director picked up his soda can, found it empty and reached over to take hers. "I hate it when you start making impossible things sound sensible.'' He gulped down what was left of her soda. "All right. The job's yours and you can have Gorman and Martinez.''

"And you,'' she added, with a satisfied smile.

"Huh? Oh, no. I already told you, we're overscheduled. You can work around the clock if you want to, but not me.''

Kate stretched her arms wide in entreaty. "What else have you got to do with your free time? You're a bachelor—"

"No thanks to this place. Kate, I met someone and—well, you might be content to spend your free time with a half ton of horseflesh, but I prefer two-legged company. Just how many women do you think are out there who have a weakness for chubby, red-haired boys? Boy—heck, I'm thirty! Time's a wasting. Soon women will be chasing me away with a broom and calling me a dirty old man."

"You were born a dirty old man," Kate drawled, her smile affectionate. "And I've told you before, I have nothing against dating. I just don't care to be paraded before all the single men in Atlanta like breeding stock to be auctioned off to the highest bidder."

"Oh, the woes of the wealthy," Rusty complained in falsetto, placing the back of his hand against his forehead. "Cotillion balls, azalea balls, charity balls...party, party, party. It's more than a girl should be asked to endure."

Kate ripped a sheet of paper off her clipboard, scrunched it up and tossed it at him, hitting his broad chest. "Are you going to help me or am I going to have to blackmail you?"

"I suppose somebody's going to have to keep you in line. Besides, just the prospect of seeing you with a hammer in your h—ello. What's this?"

At his wide-eyed look, Kate swung around to see their receptionist and girl Friday, Sally, walk into Rusty's cramped office with a long florist's box. Kate glanced back at Rusty and whistled softly. "What were you saying about this new lady in your life?"

"It's not for him," Sally said, placing the box on Kate's lap.

Rusty gave a hoot and clapped his hands. "You should see the look on your face, Beaumont."

Kate shot him a quelling look before giving her attention to the box. She didn't need to read the gold-lettered label attached to the red satin bow to know the delivery had come from one of the best florists in town, just as she didn't need to look for a card to know who had initiated the order.

But it didn't make sense, she thought, frowning as she fingered the ribbon. A man doesn't send flowers to a woman who's clearly signaling him to leave her alone. Then again, Giles Channing seemed to be particularly immune to rejection.

Technically, she'd never accepted when he stipulated she had to go out with him in order to get the agreement signed by her father. Even now she had no intention of changing her mind. The very idea was absurd. She thought he would get the hint when he left her all those messages and she'd failed to respond. She supposed the only way to finally get her point across would be to return the flowers.

But what a shame, for if she had one weakness aside from her passion for food, it was flowers. Maybe it wouldn't hurt to take one peak, she decided, carefully sliding the ribbon off the box. *Then* she would return them.

Roses. The scent reached her even before she could set down the lid and part the green wax-paper covering. Long stemmed and a deep velvety red, they were breathtaking; but her wistful sigh was drowned out by Sally's exclamation and Rusty's whistle, as her associates moved in to take a closer look.

"Wow, Kate," Sally said, reverently fingering one of the perfect buds. "I didn't even know you were seeing someone special. Some people have all the luck."

Just as Kate was about to make a flippant reply, she spotted the glove placed across the stems. Her heart made a strange little jolt as it accelerated into a higher gear. It was a man's riding glove, superbly crafted from soft, natural leather.

"Well, how strange," Sally murmured. "What do you suppose it means?"

"Hernandez, you gotta stop watching *Sesame Street* with those kids of yours," Rusty drawled, reaching for it. "Don't you recognize kinky when you see it?"

Kate swatted his hand away and grabbed up the glove herself, only to see a note slip out. Though they all reached for it at once, she managed to grab it, warning them off with a narrow-eyed look. "And there'll be no peeking over my shoulder, is that clear?" she added archly.

"Killjoy," Rusty mumbled. But he circled back to his own chair while Sally had to run back to her desk to answer the phone.

Kate unfolded the white sheet of stationery. Personalized stationery, she realized, noting the embossed letters *GQC* in the top left-hand corner. Even though she'd already guessed who it was from, she felt her heartbeat increase again. It shifted into overdrive when she read the contents.

I'll pick you up this evening. Seven sharp.

She didn't know whether to laugh or swear.

The man had style, she would give him that. The glove was a gauntlet, just as she'd suspected. Realizing he couldn't force her to go with him, he was challenging her to refuse him, as if they were opponents on some field of honor. Oh, how she would like to meet that challenge. But the days of dueling went out of style with hoop skirts and black-powder pistols, and that left her in an unpleasant fix.

Then she smiled. Maybe they weren't gone—exactly. There was more than one way to skin a cat. Wasn't it the colonists who learned from the Indians how best to fight the Redcoats? Giles Channing would have his dinner companion, and she who laughed last might even send him a potted lily in consolation.

Across the desk Rusty drew his head into his brawny shoulders like a turtle seeking cover. "Uh-oh. I know that look. Listen, Kate, I'm not going to ask what's in that note. Just promise you aren't about to do anything drastic?"

Kate blinked and gave him her most guileless smile. "Don't be silly. I'm merely going out to dinner."

She was almost late because finding the perfect dress took forever, and then she got stuck in evening traffic. By the time she arrived at her apartment, she had just enough time to shower, blow dry her hair and get dressed. But when the doorbell announced his arrival precisely at seven, she grinned at her reflection in the bathroom mirror and knew she'd succeeded in capturing the right look. Placing an expression of beatific repose on her face, she went to answer the door.

All she lacked, Giles thought moments later, was a choir of angels singing something by Brahms. Angels and an aureole accenting the garland of freesia already haloing her head.

He took it all in—the squeaky clean hair, the freshly scrubbed face, the white, floral embroidered shift that despite its simplicity seemed to enhance her willowy figure, the matching hose and ballet slippers—and could almost feel the bite of his riding glove on his freshly shaved cheek. Not only had she surprised him by actually being here, she was daring him to take out the epitome of every vestal virgin sacrifice in every gladiator B-movie ever made. Touché, Giles mused, and now what?

Glancing down to the bouquet of daisies he'd brought her, he plucked several petals from one blossom and tossed them into the air. "Hail MGM and United Artists. I come to bury Caesar, not to praise him," he drawled as the petals showered over their shoulders.

"Hello," she murmured, determined not to be amused. She dropped her gaze from the dashing image he presented in his navy suit, intent on remaining unattracted, as well, and considered the remaining daisies. "More flowers. You're too kind."

He eyed her suspiciously, but gave her a courtly bow as he handed them to her. "There was a vendor outside my hotel, I couldn't resist."

Kate lowered her head over the daisies, repressing a chuckle. It pleased her that she'd knocked him off balance. But she wanted him bored to tears. Before this was over, she hoped he would be. "Won't you come in while I put these in water? I'll only be a minute."

Giles watched her disappear into the kitchen before glancing around to study her apartment. It was small, a far cry from the opulence of Meadowbrook, but cozy. The walls were ivory, the furniture a light pine, the couch and chairs rattan with green-plaid cushions. Framed photographs of her family were scattered everywhere. It all reminded him of his late grandmother's summer home in Hastings; but though he'd loved that place, he now found himself feeling caged. Shaking off the odd reaction, he turned to study the numerous awards from her years in equitation.

"We can go now if you like."

He turned to see her standing in the kitchen doorway, sedate, her hands clasped around a small white purse.

Lovely, but he would have preferred her to come out swinging and damning him to the devil. At least he knew how to react to that. "Yes—er—of course."

He escorted her to his Jaguar and she politely thanked him for getting the door for her. When he got in the driver's side, she complimented him on his taste in vehicles. When he asked her how her day had been, she dismissed the question with a tinkling laugh that made him wince and insisted she would much prefer hearing how *his* day had gone.

Before they'd driven more than a mile, he knew if the charade continued, he was going to cheerfully strangle her. For a man who had a natural abhorrence for violence, that was saying a lot. "How long do you plan to keep this up?" he asked as he stopped the car for a traffic light.

She adjusted the air-conditioner vent to blow directly on her. Already her textured hose were beginning to feel unbearably hot. "Why, whatever do you mean?" she asked, her voice oozing honey.

"That's what I thought."

Did she really think he was going to take this lying down? He'd merely asked her to fulfill her part of an agreement. Damn it all, he'd been a *gentleman*, hadn't he?

When the light turned green, he shifted into first and accelerated. All right, he decided, gripping the head of the gear shift with renewed determination. If it was games she wanted, games she would get.

Spotting a phone booth about a half a block away, he eased into the right lane, then pulled into the parking lot of a service station. Excusing himself, he climbed out. "I've just remembered a call I have to make," he said, already reaching into his pocket for change.

Watching him leave, Kate almost purred with pleasure. He was going to *pretend* to make a call, she assured herself, barely able to contain her glee. When he returned, he was going to be excruciatingly apologetic. Something had come up, a crisis that no one could handle but him. He would assure her that he would make it up to her. Fat chance she would let him. As far as she was concerned this settled all debts.

Kate was nearly bouncing in her seat with excitement when he returned. "Sorry," he murmured, refastening his seat belt.

"Oh, I understand," Kate said, giving him the most understanding smile she could summon. "Duty calls. We'll do it another time."

"I beg your pardon?"

"You're being called back to the office, aren't you?"

"Whatever gave you that idea?"

"Well, you—I thought—" She caught the glimmer of amusement in his eyes and all her hope and enthusiasm was snuffed out like a candle doused by a tub of ice water. She slumped back in her seat. "Nothing," she mumbled dejectedly.

Inordinately pleased with himself, Giles eased the car back into traffic. Let her brood, he thought. It wouldn't last. Just as soon as they reached their destination, she would have plenty to say. His only regret was that the cracked crab and Dom Perignon he'd been looking forward to would have to wait for another day.

Five minutes later he pulled into the parking lot of the Azalea Plaza Bowling Lanes. It cost him not to wince when he parked between the pick-up with the Confederate flag draped across the rear window and the jalopy whose bumper was held on by wire. But seeing Kate's open-mouthed stare made it worth it.

"Here we are," he said cheerfully as he killed the engine.

"You don't seriously expect me to go in there like this?"

"My dear, remember we have a deal. That is unless you're chickening out, as you Yanks say."

Kate closed her eyes and tried to remember how to count to ten in French. All she could remember were a few choice Italian slurs a finishing-school roommate taught her. She wondered if the penalty for decking an earl-once-removed was more severe than committing aggravated assault on a common citizen. She wondered if there was any way to get out of this without ending up looking like a fool—or a quitter. Finding none, she unsnapped her seat belt and shot him a look she'd seen Elizabeth use on overbearing maître d's.

"Of course, not. I was—I was simply waiting for you to get the door."

She told herself she could handle it. Even when they walked into the noisy building and a little girl pointed at them declaring in a voice a mezzo soprano would envy, "Mommy, mommy—are those people just married?" Even when they walked up to the front desk and the balding man in a Hawaiian-print shirt snickered, yelled, "Yo—garçon!" and directed the floor attendant to show them to the best lane in the house and not to forget to leave the wine list. And even when the attendant returned with the scuffed, bent-toed bowling shoes they were told they would have to rent in order to play.

But she vowed revenge. She didn't know how and she didn't know when, but she would make sure he got his. By the time she was through with him, Giles Channing was going to think the Egyptians got off light with plagues of frogs and grasshoppers.

"Would you like to take that practice shot the attendant said we were entitled to?" Giles asked solicitously, interrupting her scheming.

Kate got up and shuffled over to the ball rack to pick up the ball she'd chosen. Sliding her fingers into the three holes, she hoisted the heavy globe off the rack. But her grip was poor and the ball heavy; it dropped with a resounding thud, missing her right foot by an inch.

She heard a choking sound behind her that sounded suspiciously like laughter, but she chose to ignore it. In her current mood, she didn't trust herself. Anyway, wasn't the prerequisite to being a successful murderess making sure there were no witnesses?

"Perhaps two hands might be advisable," Giles called out.

Kate bent to pick up the ball, found her narrow skirt wouldn't accommodate the move and shimmied her hips slightly until it slid high enough above the knee to allow her to stoop. Then, casting a malevolent glare over her shoulder, she shuffled down the aisle in her too-large shoes and flung the ball from the cradle of her linked hands.

"Hey, lady!" the beer-bellied man beside her shouted, as her ball bounced into his lane and slowly plopped into the left gutter. "We're trying to have a league game here. Do you mind?"

She endured three games before Giles suggested they call it a night. It was dark when they exited the bowling alley and her head was pounding. Whether the pain came because she could still hear bowling balls crashing into pins in her head or because she was famished was a moot point.

"All in all I'd say we did rather well," Giles said when they were settled in his car. "I really started to rack up points after that fellow explained the purpose of those dots painted on the floor."

Kate shot him a sidelong look. "A score of fifty-six is hardly anything to write home about."

"Well, it beat your eleven, didn't it?"

She gave him an imperious sniff and pushed the slipping garland of freesia up off her forehead. "I'm starving."

"Surely not. After those two king-sized beers and that foot-long hot dog?"

And Elizabeth called him a gentleman? Ha. Kate turned to look out the passenger's window, leaving the choice of restaurants up to him. All she knew was that when they got there, she was going to order the biggest, most expensive steak in the place.

But minutes later she was startled to discover they were pulling into her apartment parking lot. Speechless, she could only stare at him.

"I'll walk you up," he said amiably.

She went, but only because she was temporarily speechless.

Her apartment was on the second floor and they made the trip in silence. When they reached her door and she slid the key into the lock, she'd recovered somewhat. Enough to be prepared to turn him down if he asked to come in for a nightcap or coffee. But again he surprised her by simply saying good-night.

She was certain her mouth fell open. "That's it?"

It had been the plan, he told himself. But now, standing there in the soft glow of lamplight and moonlight, seeing the way she tilted her head back to gaze at him, the light enhancing her flushed face and wide eyes, he couldn't resist the impulse that rose like an irrepressible flood.

"Maybe not," he drawled, sliding a hand around the back of her neck and propelling her toward him. "Not quite."

It seemed to take forever for his mouth to claim hers. Plenty of time for her to react, to reject. She could see the question, the expectation that she would in his eyes. And then it was happening and there was only the moment and the feeling.

He was no less careful than the last time, his expertise no less precise. Kate knew she would be making a gigantic mistake to let it happen again and pushed against his chest, even while her mouth clung to his. But it was too little too late and within seconds her senses seemed overwhelmed by his touch, his taste. Kissing him was like imbibing a potent drink, he went straight to her head, but the resulting moan dragged from her was lost in the night breeze. Just as well—had her life depended on it, she wouldn't have been able to say whether it was a sound made in protest or desire.

But Giles knew and it filled him with a sense of triumph and wanting. He wanted to throw back his head and laugh, he wanted to sweep her into his arms and carry her inside. He would have settled for urging her back against the door and pressing his body against the supple, sleek curves of hers. Only the reminder of who she was, whose daughter she was and what all that could mean, kept him from doing so. Things had gone far enough. Anything more would create complications he had no intentions of dealing with.

It took her a moment to register his withdrawal. When she did, she only saw his eyes, those pale pantherlike eyes glittering down at her with some unfathomable message.

"Now we're through," he murmured, huskily, almost regretfully. Feeling the growing impulse to drag her back into his arms and finish what he'd started, he turned on his heel and walked away.

Kate stood there for a moment feeling as if she'd been slapped. But she quickly recovered and, not wanting him to reach his car and see her still standing there, she hurried inside, slamming the apartment door behind her.

Wretch...creep...rat! Never had she detested anyone more than Giles Channing!

Yet even before the declaration was more than a thought, her subconscious mocked her.

Do you now? Then why did you let him kiss you, and why did you kiss him back?

Exhaling with a hiss, Kate went to find some aspirin.

Four

———

"What do you mean you want to cancel the idea for the waterfall in the lobby of my hotel?" Teddy glowered at the two other men in his Omni International Building office. "It's in the plans. You drew it in," he added, pointing a finger across his desk at Steve Nolan.

Steve squirmed, but beside him Giles lifted a hand in reassurance. "Plans are subject to change, you know that. At any rate, I did warn you about my reservations. The concept's been handled splendidly in New York and I'm more certain than ever that you'd only be accused of mimicry. Nor will your alternate idea of using the city's civic symbol work. I've checked around and there's already at least two fine sculptures of the Phoenix in town. What we want to do is create something unique that would make the Beaumont Hotel stand out among other hotels in the country, even in the world." As he rose, he gestured to Steve with his Cross pen. "Show him the sketches of the aquarium idea."

"Fish!" Teddy flattened his hands on his desk blotter to stop his rocking and sputtered. "You want me to replace a majestic waterfall with a tank of goldfish?"

"Not just a tank. Not goldfish," Steve Nolan replied, pushing his glasses up the bridge of his nose before sliding the detailed artwork toward Teddy. "We're talking about a series of structures that will stretch throughout the lobby. They would be linked in a series of three or four geometric patterns creating attractive seating areas. Studies have shown there's a soothing factor in . . ."

Giles wandered over to the window and let Steve sell the idea. Lifting a hand to the back of his neck, he massaged the muscles there, not at all surprised to find them knotted. Why shouldn't they be when he hadn't had a decent night's sleep in days. The irritating thing was that it didn't have so much to do with the pressures of the job or with adjusting to the new apartment he'd moved into over the weekend as it did with women. Specifically one woman, he amended, glancing down to see the Omni Complex and arena below. One woman and his inability to keep her out of his thoughts.

As if drawn by some magnet, Giles once again shifted his gaze to Teddy's credenza, to one of the two silver-and-gold framed photographs proudly displayed there.

Kate, he thought with an inner sigh, studying the face that grinned back at him in a way that mirrored all the energy and optimism of youth. He needed her to distract him the way London needed more fog.

What was it about her that drew him? Granted, she was attractive, but she was also somewhat younger than the women he normally dated. Not to mention overtly outspoken. Unpredictable.

Irresistible.

He frowned slightly. It had been five days since that fiasco of a date and still he couldn't lay the memory of it to rest. It wasn't their foolish attempts at one-upmanship he kept dwelling on, either. Of course, he had no regrets about that; he wasn't so old that he didn't know how to have a good laugh or two. But he should never have touched her again.

That first kiss in the stables had been potent enough. The second had left him feeling as if something had clawed at him from the inside trying to get out. His past liaisons had always brought out the best in him—care, affection, even humor—enjoyable feelings, but none he couldn't walk away from.

He wasn't sure that once having made love with Kate, he could walk away from her. He didn't want to find out.

"And is that your opinion, too, Channing?" Teddy demanded.

"Hmm? Indeed. Adding push-button audio recordings in each unit to describe the exotic species would not only be educational, but marvelous entertainment for youngsters while they wait for their parents to—"

A knock at the door interrupted him. In the next instant Kate walked in, making Giles forget whatever else he'd been about to say.

"Hi, Daddy, is it all right if—oh." Realizing her father wasn't alone and *who* he was with, she began to withdraw. "Thelma was away from her desk. I'll come back later."

"You will not," Teddy declared, pushing himself out of his chair. Hurrying over to her, he wrapped his strong arms around her for a giant bear hug. "You don't visit me nearly enough as it is. My, don't you look pretty enough to sit on top of a wedding cake."

Repressing a groan, Kate cast a furtive glance toward Giles. Of all the luck, she thought. At least he didn't look any more pleased about this than she was. "I'm sorry for interrupting. I only wanted to get your signature approving the plumber's estimate on the renovation site."

"Yes, yes, but you can still come in and say hello." He drew her toward the other two men. "You already know Giles, but you didn't have a chance to meet Steve Nolan the other day when—er, Steve, this is my baby, Kate."

As the two shook hands and exchanged pleasantries, Giles collected his scattered wits. Dear God, she looked lovely, he thought. Her short-sleeved, double-breasted jacket was lavender, her pleated skirt white, and with her hair held off her temples by barrettes, she looked as fresh as a spring flower.

"Good to see you again, Katherine," he murmured, something inside him needing her to acknowledge him.

Her own greeting was even more low-key and she barely spared him a glance before turning back to her father. "Would you like me to leave this and pick it up later? I'm in something of a hurry myself."

"What? We were about to go to lunch. Channing hasn't seen the view from the Sun Dial yet, so I thought we'd go over to the Peachtree. Why don't you join us?"

Kate could almost feel Giles's eyes on her and it made it all the more difficult to make her answering smile look regretful. Go to lunch with him? She wouldn't be able to swallow a bite. "I'm sorry, Daddy, but I have my own plans. I'm lunching with Ted Vandergriff."

Her father's delighted look over the fact that she actually had a date quickly turned into one of indignation. "Over my dead body. Vandergriff? The Piedmont Nurseries Vandergriff? Girl, he's married!"

Kate pursed her lips and reached up to adjust the knot on his brown-and-gold tie. "Thank you for pointing that out to me, you old grumble bear. I've only been giving his eldest daughter dressage lessons for two months, remember? I'm taking him to lunch because I want to talk him into donating the landscaping for our new park."

Clearly relieved, Teddy laughingly declared Vandergriff didn't stand a chance and opened the folder Kate passed him. Beside him, Giles waged an internal battle with conflicting emotions. Why, when he should be relieved that she, too, was trying to act as though there was nothing between them, did he feel disappointed? It was what he wanted, wasn't it?

Yet he found himself regretting that she'd declined her father's invitation, envious of the man named Vandergriff and annoyed. Did she think she could really get away with treating him as if he were nothing more than an annoying fly that had somehow snuck in where it wasn't welcome?

Deciding his reactions were absurd, he excused himself, muttering something about remembering a chart he needed in his office. It was a lie, of course, but once outside he did wander over to the offices he'd leased on the same floor. He thought he might kill some time by checking his phone messages.

After about ten minutes, when he estimated he'd given Kate enough time to get her signature and leave, he made his way back to Teddy's office.

Neither Giles nor Kate were looking up when they rounded the corner by the elevators. Giles reacted more quickly, but even so he nearly flattened her.

"Blast—sorry about that," he said, grabbing her arms to steady her as her folder shot out of her hands and papers flew everywhere. The brush of her hair, soft as a kiss across the backs of his hands made him itch to stroke it. Without consciously thinking of it, he inhaled and caught a hint of flowers—lily of the valley. He'd never noticed her wearing a fragrance before. Had she been entirely truthful to her father about her luncheon being all business?

"Excuse me," she said stiffly. "I should have been looking where I was going."

They stooped simultaneously to collect the scattered papers. Their knees almost touched. Their hands did, and Kate pulled back as if the brief contact had scorched her. Though she quickly hid her reaction by grabbing at the folder, Giles looked up at her.

It was another mistake. Her movements caused the neckline of her jacket to gape slightly and gave him a beguiling view of flawless skin, provocative curves and feminine lace, bringing back the memory of how good it felt to hold her and how much more he'd been tempted to do.

"Kate," he murmured, giving up his internal battle. "How have you been?"

He had nerve, she thought, snatching the last of the papers out of his hand and stuffing them into her folder. How did he think she was? Every time she found herself in the man's presence he was either humiliating her or, at the least, causing her no end of problems.

"Once I get out of here, I'll be just—" The rest of her speech was lost as she lifted her head and found herself looking straight into his dark-fringed eyes, eyes that were intense and shadowed with—regret? The power of them, of him, made her feel a restless churning inside, and not a little fear.

"Leave me alone," she whispered.

"What makes you think I'm not trying?"

"You enjoy toying with me."

"Do I?" He wasn't sure "toying" was the correct term for what he enjoyed most when it came to her. He dropped his gaze to her lips, lightly colored with pink lip gloss. It would only take the slightest effort to close the distance between them and absorb her warmth, her taste, and to sate a little of the gnawing hunger he was beginning to recognize whenever he was around her.

"Try it and I swear I'll bite."

He was almost grateful to her for jerking him back to the land of the sane. He was even able to indulge in a low chuckle as he lightly chucked her under her chin.

"Ah, Kate. As much as I hate to admit it, I've missed you."

"No need to purge your soul to me." Clutching her folder to her chest she stood. "I've never advocated confession being beneficial to anyone except the suicidal."

A likely comment to come from a kitten who's already used up several of her nine lives, Giles thought, rising, also. He gave her a crooked smile. "Now don't try to convince me that you haven't thought of me even once?"

"Ah, *thought*. Well, yes, that is different, isn't it? But I managed to solve that problem, too. I simply cut a picture of you out of the *Atlanta Constitution*."

"Why I'm touched."

"And tacked it to the dart board in my office. Hold please," she called to someone behind him. Then she skirted around him to catch the elevator being held for her.

Giles reached up to finger his tie and he cleared his throat. That should teach him to leave well enough alone. He wanted a reason to stay away from her? She was giving him one. Dart board, indeed. Well, let the little hellion sink her claws into someone else's hide. He'd never had to chase a woman in his life, and he certainly wasn't going to start now.

But as the days progressed and one week slipped into the next, Giles discovered that he could protest all he wanted. The fact remained that Kate wasn't someone to dismiss easily—and every time he saw her, his attraction grew.

They ran into each other everywhere, at Teddy's office, on the job site, at this party or that event. Even when he took a Saturday morning off to indulge in a relaxing ride at Meadowbrook, she would be there in the ring practicing her dressage and jumps on Zulu.

The first time their paths crossed there, he chose not to pursue a conversation, convincing himself that it was what he wanted. But on the following Saturday, all his determination was forgotten when he was taking a leisurely ride on one of the trails and she came from nowhere on her devilish mount, charging past and almost unseating him. He might have let it go, simply declaring her certifiable, but then he heard her laugh.

It was too much. He took off in hot pursuit.

It was ridiculous, considering the difference in their horses. His was a respectable gelding aptly named Goodboy Hank, but hardly a match for the stallion. It was only due to Kate eventually slowing Zulu to a walk that allowed Giles to catch up with her.

"You think you're quite amusing don't you?" he demanded when he drew up beside her on the wooded trail that separated Meadowbrook's sprawling pastures.

She allowed a faint smile, but kept looking straight ahead toward the break in the tree line. "I was simply giving Zulu his lead as I'd promised so he could run off some of his energy. If I'd penned him after all that dressage, he would have kicked down the stables. I see you found a mount suitable to your—talents."

"We don't all have a death wish," he replied archly, trying not to notice that her beauty seemed that much more enhanced when she was excited. Her aqua T-shirt perfectly matched the scarf tied around her hair and both were the same color as her eyes, the same color as the Mediterranean in the height of summer. Giles dragged his gaze away to glance around him. "Besides, part of the benefit of riding a well-disciplined horse is being able to enjoy the passing scenery."

"Then you're right to give up your idea of trying Zulu."

Giles brought up the gelding. "I didn't say that. You're more likely to deny me the opportunity than I am to decline it."

Kate eased the reluctant stallion around. Her smile was almost wicked. "You think so? You're old enough to take foolish gambles and not complain when it comes time to pay the price."

"You think I can't stay on him."

"I told you, he isn't fond of men."

"Obviously explaining your attachment."

Kate's smile turned brittle. Without further comment, she gracefully dismounted.

Recognizing yet another challenge, Giles did the same.

"What, no words of warning?" he drawled, as she handed him Zulu's reins. "No sermon for survival?"

Her answering chuckle was as subtle as the touching of blades at the start of a fencing match. She held the stallion steady as Giles mounted and adjusted the stirrups to suit his longer legs. Finally, she eased alongside him. The glint in her eyes was undeniably feline.

"Enjoy your ride, Lord Channing," she said, slapping Zulu briskly on the thigh.

Clearly not at all pleased with the change in riders or the slap, Zulu took off with the exact lunge of speed Kate had expected. He headed straight out into the open pasture, quickly accelerating to a breakneck speed.

Now she would see what his lordship was made of, Kate thought, collecting Hank's reins and walking him a ways. She let him go by a great old oak tee and breathed in the scent of sun-warmed grass. Shielding her eyes with her hand, she could see Giles—bent low over Zulu's neck—disappear behind the eastern boundary of the woods. She would give him fifteen minutes and if he wasn't back by then, she supposed she would have to go look for him. Sometimes Zulu was more amenable once he'd had his run. But he could also stay muleheaded.

Ten minutes, she amended, checking her watch.

Damn, maybe she'd made a mistake. She didn't really want to see Giles hurt. It was just that he was so irritatingly sure of himself. It was his fault that he'd provoked her into wanting to wipe that confident smile off his face.

She wouldn't have let him on Zulu at all if he hadn't made that crack about her sharing the stallion's attitude toward the male gender. She didn't hate men, she just didn't believe in primping for them, simpering around them or making herself available whenever they crooked their fingers. Any man who wanted her would have to meet her on equal ground. Giles Channing would never conform to that criteria.

She'd read enough about him in the papers, in *Atlanta*, their monthly magazine, and even in cosmopolitan national magazines. He liked his women glamorous, accommodating and smart enough to know that any gestures of affection he might reward them with wouldn't necessarily include a gold band. However, considering the ever-changing faces in those photos, she surmised it wasn't doing much to hurt his popularity. Obviously there were those who were operating under the illusion that *they* might be the one to capture his heart and win him forever.

Well, there was no way she was going to get caught up in that three-ring circus, she assured herself, resting a shoulder against the massive tree truck. She would just as soon put her money on a lottery ticket than bet on him settling down with one woman, or at least one whose heritage wasn't as deeply rooted in English tradition as his was.

Yet she had to admit the man had charisma.... She sighed inwardly, remembering how dashing he'd looked with his navy polo shirt and dove-gray riding breeches; he *was* one of the most handsome men she'd ever seen. But, damn it all, that didn't mean she wanted to be attracted to him.

She kicked a dried limb that had fallen from the tree.

There, she'd admitted it. Now she could put it behind her. She was human. She could acknowledge that she had desires and needs just like any other healthy woman, and maybe he was particularly talented at reminding her of that. But it didn't mean she was going to do anything about it. Giles Channing was only here to build her father's center, then he would be off to chase another rainbow.

Still, it wouldn't hurt to ease up on him a little, she decided, thinking about the needling she'd been giving him since his arrival. After all, hadn't he helped her sway her father into helping with her ABA project? And the trip to the bowling alley *had* been funny—once she'd gotten over being furious with him.

As she spotted him coming back around the tree line, still bent close to Zulu's neck, she couldn't repress the giggle that rose up her throat, though she wasn't ready to admit it was partly from relief. When he was closer and she saw the disarray of his hair and that he was apparently unhurt, the giggle turned to helpless laughter.

He successfully brought up the stallion not far from where Hank was grazing. Zulu tossed his head and whinnied as if rebuking Kate for allowing this in the first place. Pale beneath his tan, Giles cautiously eased himself out of the saddle.

"Well, look at it this way," Kate said, wiping a tear from her eye with the back of her index finger. "At least you managed to stay on him. You did manage to stay on, didn't you?"

Giles *managed* not to wince as he raked his hands through his windblown hair. By morning, he knew every muscle in his body would be aching from fighting that devil.

"You know perfectly well if I hadn't, he'd have left me to walk back to the stables."

"No, he would have come to me. I did warn you, you know."

She was irresistible when she laughed and, with the sun peeking through the tree to ignite the shades of silver and gold in her hair, Giles found his tumultuous emotions finding a new outlet in desire. He knew it was crazy, but if anyone was to blame, it was her. She was bewitching him.

"Yes," he murmured, taking a step closer. "So you did. The question remains, who's going to warn me about you?"

Kate's backward step was instinctive. There was nothing threatening in his eyes, and yet she could feel a change between them. Her laughter ebbed to a breathless wheeze. "Me? I didn't force you to ride him."

"You dared me." He took another step, smiling when her backward one matched his. "The challenge was clear, and if there's anything you and I seem to recognize best in each other, sweet Kate, it's the fascination with challenge.''

Her heart plummeted as she recognized the gleam of intent in his eyes. She'd roused the panther and he'd awakened hungry. Worse, she found herself backed up against the ancient oak. As he took another step closer and rested one hand against the trunk near her head, she knew her options were seeping away faster than spring rain on parched ground. But he was right about her; she wasn't one to turn from a challenge.

She lifted her chin and looked straight into his eyes. "So what now? Is this where you try to seduce me?"

He lifted the end of her sheer scarf and inhaled the alluring scent of her shampoo. "No. This is where you remind me that I'm stepping out on a high wire with no net below." He released the scarf and trailed the backs of his fingers along her cheek. "And that I'm taking you with me."

She closed her eyes as his fingers discovered the pulse beat at the base of her throat and his warm breath tickled her ear. "Doesn't it matter to you that I don't like you?" she whispered.

"Just when I consider that only Napoleon started out with worse odds—but look how far he got."

Her lips twitched. "All right, I don't want to like you."

"No. But you want me, don't you?" he murmured, touching his lips to the flawless skin between her eyebrows. He glanced down and saw her lips part, the tip of her pink tongue slip out and moisten her lips. He cupped her chin and with his thumb he stroked that silken moistness. "Yes, you do," he sighed. "And God help us both for that."

His lips were firm but undemanding against hers, somehow knowing she would have fought him if it had been any different. He gave her a chance to feel and need, slowly beginning to coax with tiny, nibbling kisses that were more tempting than satisfying. She tried not to want, but her body betrayed her. Her lips parted, her head lifted to seek more and, when he still denied her the complete kiss she craved, she reached up to grasp the hair at his nape and brought him closer.

His groan of satisfaction was muffled by the pressure of his lips against hers. No longer hesitant, he traced her lips and teeth with his tongue and almost groaned again when hers twined with his. But gentle was their exploration and just as gently he trailed his fingers over her lithe body, down her throat, over her breast. Her sigh was as fragile as the tiny bud that thrust eagerly through her clothing pressing against his palm, and he knew he wanted to see it, see her, with nothing but the sun and his body to warm her. He wanted her slender limbs wrapped around him, drawing him closer to the heat he felt smoldering within her. Sliding his hands down to her hips, he pressed her against the tree with his body, revealing his growing vulnerability to her.

Kate felt her body heat, liquify. She stretched and drew him closer, wanting more of the feeling, of him. Power and need mingled together. She felt the urge to laugh, cry and please. So many emotions, all of them new and brought out by a man who was all wrong for her.

"Kate...I want you," he rasped, dragging his lips from hers and burying his face in her hair. "I know it's insane. I know we've done nothing but butt heads from the moment we met. Maybe it's because these emotions between us were struggling to find the right outlet." In an attempt to slow things down, he cupped her face with his hands and lifted it for sweet, light kisses on her forehead, nose and chin. "Let's go somewhere where we can be alone. My place—"

"No."

"All right, then your place."

He didn't understand. She didn't herself. How in God's name had she gotten herself into this mess? Shaking her head to clear away the smoke and fireworks, she pulled away from him and rubbed her arms as if cold. Somehow he'd managed to get under her defenses and make her want him even though he represented exactly the type of man she'd always tried to avoid. As she turned away, she didn't know who she was more angry with, herself or him.

He came up behind her and stroked her hair, confused by her withdrawal. Could it be that she was shy when it came to the subject of sex? Could she be less experienced than he'd guessed? "Kate, would it help to know that as much as I want you, I'd be a patient and gentle lover?"

"I suppose you've had enough practice to perfect your technique?"

"I beg your pardon?"

"Thanks for the offer, but I don't think I care to become another notch in your bedpost."

Giles stiffened against the surprise and hurt, but gratefully anger came quickly. He'd never apologized for his affection for women, nor would he begin now; but neither would he tolerate her insinuating that he was indiscriminate.

"I see." Straightening to an almost military stiffness, he drew a calming breath. He could hear the hurt in his voice and cursed himself for not being able to hide it. "Obviously an apology is in order. It was clearly an impropriety on my part to assume that you'd felt the same things I did. Be assured that I won't burden you with my offensive advances again, Miss Beaumont."

He collected Hank. Leaping up into the saddle, he rode off without sparing her another glance.

Kate watched him go, torn between relief and shame. She was certain she'd done the right thing in stopping this before it had gone further; however, she hadn't expected it to hurt so.

Most of all, never would she have expected the over-powering urge to ride after him and apologize.

Five

"I'm glad you agreed to come with me tonight."

Kate settled back in the plush seat of the limousine and gave her sister an amused look. "Agreed? You threatened to sign me up to model in your ladies' club's fall fashion show if I didn't. What choice did I have?"

"Unless I can find another size-four model, you're not off the hook yet." She waved away Kate's protest and continued. "I also appreciate that you'd have preferred to skip the opening night cocktail party and just attend the musical. But being a patron for the summer series, you know how Dad felt about having the family represented, especially since he had to attend that symposium in Tampa."

Disgruntled at the thought of still being on her sister's list, Kate crossed her arms and grimaced. "Symposium my foot. Three weeks ago at the opening of *Evita* he conveniently got called away to Dallas on business. What do you want to bet he's on a private yacht somewhere playing poker with his old cronies?'' The thought made Kate grin, especially when she considered how useful the information might be if she needed an edge in a future negotiation of some kind with her father.

Elizabeth had a problem keeping her own lips from twitching, ''Don't you dare repeat that theory to anyone else tonight.''

''Really, Liz. Do you think anyone would be surprised?''

''That's beside the point. Just remember you've been waiting for *Into the Woods* to go on tour since it opened on Broadway.'' Elizabeth gave into the smile as she again eyed her younger sister's attire. ''With that dress you could be in the cast.''

Kate glanced down at herself. The white-and-rose floral print had princess sleeves and a ribbed bodice that ended in several tiers of skirt. ''Are you sure it's not too much? The saleslady at that boutique you recommended said it was the latest style, but I'm not sure . . . I feel like a flamenco dancer.'' She enviously eyed Elizabeth's subdued moss-green sheath. The only drama to it was in the starburst brooch at the juncture of the diagonally cut neckline.

''You look darling,'' Elizabeth assured her. ''Why didn't you take her advice and have your hair crimped?''

Lifting a hand up to make sure the end of her French braid was still neatly tucked up in back, Kate shot her a dry look. ''I was willing to try a partial make-over, but let's not get carried away.''

''What intrigues me is why you gave in as much as you did?'' Elizabeth picked up one of Kate's hands and lifted a finely arched eyebrow. ''The last time I saw you wear-

ing nail polish was at my wedding. There was more of it on
your panty hose than on your nails. What's going on?''

Kate snatched back her hand and hid it beneath her
purse, not wanting her sister to see that she'd done a hap-
hazard job this time, as well. "For the last ten years you've
been after me not to be such a tomboy. Finally, when I do
try to enhance my image, you're suspicious. I swear a person can't win around here."

"Let me roll down the divider window and you can try
selling that to Clarence. Kate, I know you. You're as attached to your blue jeans as Dad is to that hideous ma-
roon robe he wears when he knows he can stay in at night
and watch TV."

"What's wrong with that robe? We gave it to him for
Father's Day."

"The year I bought you your first training bra. Do you
still have *it*?" Elizabeth began to turn away, only to do a
quick double take. "Wait a minute. Why didn't I see it
before—there's a man behind all this, isn't there? I don't
believe it."

Kate frowned, not at all pleased that her interest in anyone should make her sister bubble with laughter, and less
pleased when she realized all her efforts to camouflage her
motives had been in vain. "There's no man," she said de-
fensively. "I'm simply in the mood for a change."

"Oh, Kate, I wasn't really laughing *at* you. It's just that
you've managed to avoid or discourage the attentions of
almost every eligible bachelor in our circle for so long—
you can't blame me for being surprised."

With an inner sigh, Kate glanced out the window, barely
focusing on the passing scenery. It would be senseless to
continue protesting; the question was how much to con-
fess? Maybe she'd made a mistake in coming. Chances
were that *he* wouldn't show anyway. Knowing her father,

he'd probably taken Giles with him to Tampa. But if Giles was at the theater tonight, she was hoping they might casually meet, exchange a few words, and perhaps he might see that she was trying to apologize for what she'd said that day at Meadowbrook. Surely after two weeks he'd gotten over at least some of his anger toward her.

Elizabeth watched as Kate nervously fiddled with the delicate chain on her evening bag. She reached over and covered her sister's slender hand with her own. "Why don't you tell me what all that brooding is about?"

"Liz . . . do you think I'm unforgivably witchy?"

Only the quick flutter of finely curled lashes gave away her sister's surprise. "I suppose it will be a while before Mrs. Gentry invites you to another of her parties, though dumping ambrosia salad in her precious Lydia May's lap was exactly what that silly girl deserved when she tastelessly asked how you were holding up your strapless dress. And Chester Ford deserved getting poked with your shrimp cocktail fork the time he fondled your knee under the dinner table, even though it was only that glass of champagne his wife threw at him that people remember. But what in particular brought on that question?"

"I think I did it again. I said something to someone and, irregardless of what my intentions were, I know I had no right to come right out and insult him as I did." Kate shifted restlessly. "I'd already have apologized by now, but I haven't seen him in weeks."

"He's probably off somewhere licking his wounds." Elizabeth smiled at how Kate seemed to deflate even more upon hearing that. "Could it be that my little sister is finally falling in love?"

That rallied her somewhat. "Most of the time I can barely stand the man," she declared.

"You know what they say about there being a fine line between one and the other."

"Look who's talking, Lady Perfect who married Lord Perfect. You two never exchanged a harsh—" Seeing her sister glance away, Kate grimaced for bringing up an obviously still painful subject. Or *was* she thinking of Daniel? She swung around in her seat. "Liz do you ever think of Morgan?"

"Now wait a minute," Elizabeth replied with an embarrassed laugh. "What does he have to do with all this? There was nothing between Morgan Deveroux and me. For goodness sakes, he was a stable hand."

"So what? Did it stop you from being attracted to him? It certainly didn't stop him from being obsessed with you." With a wistful sigh, Kate sat back in her seat. "I used to watch you two... it sure was better than reading those boring Victorian novels for English class."

"Kate!"

"I'll never forget the look on his face when he heard you were going to marry Daniel. Daddy was furious with him for leaving without giving any notice, but I never blamed him. Do you ever wonder how he's doing, Liz?"

"I thought we were talking about your problem?" Elizabeth asked, fiddling with her own evening bag.

Kate would have liked to pursue the subject further, but feeling the chilly wall rising between them, she shrugged. "My problem is that I haven't yet learned to think before I open my mouth."

"You won't get any arguments on that from me."

"At least you could give me some credit for wanting to change."

Elizabeth drew in a deep breath and reached over to squeeze Kate's hand. "I am, and I'm sorry. All right, you're not *that* witchy—if you want to know the truth, sometimes I envy your courage in speaking up for what you believe in. Now, are you going to tell me who this mystery man is, or do I have to guess?''

''Giles Channing,'' Kate muttered reluctantly, waiting for the incredulous laughter to begin.

After a wide-eyed look of surprise, Elizabeth did smile, but it was more a smile of realization than amusement. ''Giles. Of course, I should have seen it myself.''

''Seen what? There's nothing to see other than an overly confident and easily bored man taking an innate pleasure in irritating me whenever our paths cross.'' She glanced over, saw that her sister clearly didn't believe her and groaned. ''Will you stop looking at me like that. I tell you I'm *not* falling in love with him! I just want to straighten out a few things—all right, apologize—and then he can go to the devil for all I care.''

''You have it all planned, eh? Oh, Kate...'' Elizabeth surprised her by leaning her head back against the plush seat and closing her eyes. ''If only life worked that simply.''

''What's that supposed to mean?''

''Nothing and everything. Never mind. Just remember that I'll be around if you need me.''

At first Kate thought that he hadn't come. The banquet hall used for such occasions was crowded, but not so much that she couldn't wander from group to group and still keep an eye out for new arrivals.

Elizabeth, true to her word, stayed at her side, and Kate was grateful for the gesture of support. Elizabeth could also be counted on to carry a conversation with a corpse if she had to and directed most of their conversations, leaving Kate to scan the room and rehearse the different things she could say if Giles did happen to show.

Later she told herself that it was just like him to have come up on them from the rear. But at first she was too surprised and, amazingly, pleased. However, her pleasure soon turned to annoyance. He was with Megan Hennessey, who clung to his arm like seaweed to a pier at low tide.

"Hi, everyone," Megan gushed, flashing matching dimples. "Sorry, we're late. Giles and I were so absorbed with chatting over dinner that we lost track of time. Why, Kate, don't you look darling in that dress."

"Thank you."

"I was tempted to get something like that myself, but I've come to the conclusion I've simply outgrown the ingenue look."

Kate felt Elizabeth inch closer to her side—no doubt expecting retaliation. There was no denying the temptation was there. However, dropping her gaze to consider Megan's violet-and-pink gown, Kate decided she could afford to be generous. It looked like the curvaceous brunette had been unable to resist the dessert carts again.

She merely smiled at Megan and shifted her gaze to Giles. "Nice to see you."

He looked dashing as usual, his black suit emphasizing his lean build and aristocratic bearing. There was also no denying that it played well against his tan and his pale green eyes. She couldn't blame Megan for wanting to hold on tight, but she wondered how serious things were between them.

Sure her heart could be heard pounding against her ribs, she was grateful when Elizabeth added her own greetings and easily led them into polite small talk. Most of all she was grateful for her sister's secret, reassuring pat at the small of her back.

"Have you heard from your father?" Giles asked Elizabeth.

"He called to let us know he'd arrived safely. He'll phone again tomorrow before he heads for home."

"If you need to speak to him concerning the project, Elizabeth or I could get you the number," Kate offered politely.

"That won't be necessary. Everything is under control."

Elizabeth smoothly maneuvered the conversation toward the show they were going to see, and Kate gratefully used the opportunity to recover from the clear snub. What did she expect? It would take more than a hello to make him understand what she was trying to do. But it would help if Megan wasn't eyeing her like a watchdog protecting her property.

"I understand Gypsy foaled a filly, Kate," Megan said. "Does that mean you're going to give everyone else a chance at the charity horse show this year?" She laughed up at Giles. "I swear the way she keeps taking home the trophy, we've all accused Teddy Beaumont of buying the judges."

"Kate will be there," Elizabeth replied with a cool, regal smile. "She'll be on Zulu."

Kate could have hugged her sister. Then she saw Giles's quick frown and felt even better.

Megan dismissed the announcement with a toss of her curls. "Of all the crazy stunts...Kate, that beast is uncontrollable! I won't argue that he's not a great jumper, but you'll lose so many points in dressage—you'll never pull it off. In fact all you're liable to get for your trouble is a broken neck."

"Now, Meg. If anyone can manage him, Kate can," Giles drawled. "She's amazingly adept at cutting everything down to her size."

As Megan chuckled and agreed, Kate fought to keep her smile from wilting. She was grateful when chimes sounded announcing showtime.

People started moving toward the auditorium. Elizabeth expertly let Giles and Megan get some distance ahead before slipping her arm more firmly around her sister's waist and giving her a consoling hug.

"I'm sorry, sweetheart."

"For what? Everything's fine."

"Oh, Kate. You needn't pretend with me."

Kate managed a philosophical shrug and accepted a program from an usherette. "I wasn't expecting it to be easy."

But inside her confidence was taking a tough beating. What if he refused to hear her apology—that is if she could get him away from his "date" long enough to give it? Maybe Elizabeth could help her there. At any rate, she wasn't a quitter. Kate wouldn't accept defeat until she was out of options.

Giles was thinking of golden opportunities himself . . . like the one he hoped would come along to get him out of the theater entirely. As he and Megan took their seats, he shifted, trying to inch away from her overpowering perfume without being obvious. It was nothing like the springlike fragrance Kate had worn—*the day she'd gone out to lunch with someone else*.

He looked up to see Kate and Elizabeth slip into the row before them, two seats down. No doubt about it, he brooded; fate was a lady—one who had nothing but mischief on her mind.

It had been a whim to accept Megan's invitation to this event, and merely good manners that compelled him to take her to dinner first. Any hope of escaping now was dim, considering the construction of Beaumont Center was on schedule and had been shut down for the weekend. It looked like he was destined to spend the evening with the attractive, though self-possessed Miss Hennessey, while being acutely aware of the woman who truly fascinated him sitting only an arm's distance away. He would have preferred the drama be left to play on stage.

What was Kate up to? he wondered suspiciously. The woman he thought he was beginning to know wouldn't have let Megan get away with that admittedly catty remark about the dress, but she had. Why, and why was she being so solicitous to him? Was it simply a gesture of apology? The appeal in her eyes seemed genuinely sincere.

Yet he couldn't forget how their last meeting had ended. He wasn't the custodian to pride and image that his brother Richard, the Earl of Westridge, was; still, he couldn't deny that a certain sense of dignity ran in his blood. She'd cut deeply with her lashing remarks, and he'd felt justified in letting her know he hadn't forgotten them.

However, he could forgive her. But should he? Wouldn't it be easier in the long run to use the situation as a means to keep himself away from her?

As the house lights began to dim and the audience settled back and quieted, he glanced over to see her tilt her head to respond to something Elizabeth said. The graceful line of her neck, the delectable creaminess of her bared shoulders, made him draw in a deep breath. Just looking at her made him want.

She turned slightly and their eyes met. Captivated by their dreamy blue magic, the beckoning warmth that threatened to draw him from his seat, he would have missed applauding the rising curtain if she hadn't turned away herself.

Giles shifted again in his seat and tried to focus on the stage. All he could see was Kate on his bed with her hair in glorious disarray. It was clearly going to be a long night.

At intermission, Megan begged off Giles's offer of a glass of champagne, insisting she needed to powder her nose. He took the opportunity to seek a few moments of privacy and wandered away from the crowd to indulge in a cigar. He ended up near the entrance of the theater where there was a gallery displaying paintings of previous productions, along with signed photographs of the shows' stars. Several other people, seeming to have the same idea, roamed from display to display and he followed, though keeping his distance to avoid getting drawn into a conversation.

He told himself he wanted the time alone. When he heard the light step and soft rustle of silk behind him, he knew it wasn't quite the truth.

"That's Elizabeth's favorite," Kate said, pausing beside him to study the scene from *Camelot*. "I'm not sure whether it's because it was her first experience going to the theater at night instead of a matinee or because she loved all the pageantry in the production." She paused, waiting for him to make some kind of comment, but he remained silent. "Enjoying the show?"

"It's as charming as advertised," he replied with a negligible shrug. Though he tried not to, he drew the scent of her fragrance deep into his lungs.

She shifted to consider his profile. "You sound disappointed. Strange, since you strike me as a man who would prefer musical comedy over drama or opera."

"And we all know your insight into my preferences, as into my character, is flawless."

Kate drew in a sharp breath as pain sliced through her. How easy the words came to him, and how hard the meaning behind them. "I didn't come to argue but to apologize."

He lifted an eyebrow speculatively. "Just when I was getting used to the title of Duke of Debauchery. Oh, well, I always did say titles were more trouble than they were worth."

"I don't blame you for being angry with me."

He watched her lower her lashes to hide her disappointment—or was it hurt?—and brutally squashed the urge to take her in his arms, press kisses to those delicately veined lids, her too pale cheeks, the pulse beating a little erratically at the base of her delectable throat. Damn her, why couldn't she leave well enough alone as he was trying to do?

He flicked ashes into a nearby ashtray. "What do you want from me, Kate?"

"Nothing. I only wanted to apologize. I know what I said that day hurt you, and I know now that it was unforgivable of me to judge you on hearsay."

"And that's it?"

Kate felt embarrassment heat her cheeks, but she forced herself to meet his compelling gaze. "All right, I was hoping that maybe—maybe we could start over. Be friends."

"Friends." He purposely let his gaze drop to her breasts and lower. "I'm afraid it wouldn't work, my dear. You're a bit too much of a—distraction to ever waste on friendship and, with your father also being my business associate, you can appreciate how that puts us in a rather awkward predicament."

"Who I see is *my* business and no one else's."

Knowing he needed to end the conversation before he did something foolish, Giles turned to her fully, inching closer so that he could keep his voice low. "Shall we be lovers, Kate? Is that what you're after?" he whispered, the intensity of his look deepening the stain of color in her cheeks. "Say the word and we'll leave right now. Let the others think whatever they will. We have the weekend—longer if we suit each other even half as well as I think we would. You won't regret it. I'll make you feel things you've never dreamed of feeling with anyone else."

"Stop it!" Her voice shook with fury at his insolence. She glanced around, relieved to see that at least no one seemed to be watching.

Giles drew a slow, deep breath and crushed out his cigar, needing a moment to rein in his emotions. "Go away, Kate. As tempting as you are, I outgrew sophomoric games a long time ago."

"Why you pompous—jerk. *If* I decided I wanted you, I wouldn't need games, and you wouldn't know what hit you."

He believed it. He was already doubting his sanity for pushing her away. "Well, don't," he replied, hanging on to a thread of reason. "I'm not the man to build your dreams around."

"There you are," Megan said, coming down the hallway. As she joined them, she linked her arm through Giles's and glanced from him to Kate. "My, you two seemed to be having a serious conversation. What's going on?"

"Kate was filling me in on past productions in your fine theater. We were discussing the value of fairy tales in reality, but came to the conclusion there's a wide gulf between our philosophies."

"I don't doubt it." Megan shot Kate a patronizing smile. "She has a charming, if somewhat quixotic, view toward life in general. I'll bet you still believe in wishbones and happily ever afters, don't you, dear?"

"Once upon a time I did," Kate whispered without shifting her gaze from Giles. "But I've been cured."

Without bothering to say goodbye, she walked away.

Six

As Giles rode the elevator up to Teddy's office, he sucked in a deep breath to steady the mass of tangled nerves and frustrated emotions he'd been reduced to. He was still furious and still ashamed of himself to the point of being heartsick, and he wasn't handling either condition very well.

Women. What in heaven's name had ever made him think they were the gentler, weaker sex? With a look, one had made him want as he'd never wanted before. With a word, one had turned his life inside out. He wished he'd never laid eyes on her, but it was killing him to stay away from her. Women. *Woman*. Kate.

In the two weeks since that fiasco at the theater, they'd worked hard at avoiding each other; nevertheless, she'd somehow managed to stay in his mind. He'd tried to lose himself in his work—and what did he have to show for it? He couldn't concentrate, he couldn't eat...even his usually amiable disposition was suffering. Only yesterday he'd lost his temper with his assistant, and last week he'd harassed a secretary to the point where she'd accidentally shredded the master copy of a bid. People were beginning to whisper when he entered a room and gave him a wide berth in hallways. Hyde was taking over Jekyll, and all because of a guilty conscience.

He had been raised a gentleman, not only learning but *believing* that a woman was to be treated with a special kind of respect and care. Yet in a moment of bad judgment he'd allowed himself to be cruel to Kate, and the guilt was festering inside him like an ulcer. Professionally he accepted the need to be tough; socially he could even justify occasions where it served him to be aloof. But at heart his nature was affectionate. This vulnerability to Kate, this ridiculous loony spell he seemed to be under, had changed him and it was too much. It had to end.

It was why he was returning to Teddy's office when he would rather have stayed home. He'd accepted Teddy's invitation to join him and his daughters at an otherwise resistible reception. Giles told himself that if he could see Kate, apologize and explain why he'd been compelled to say what he did, she might forgive him. Then he might be able to forgive himself.

However, minutes later when he walked into the older man's office, Teddy and Elizabeth were indeed waiting for him, but there was no sign of Kate. "Sorry if I kept you waiting," he told them, trying to be discreet as he glanced around the room.

"Nonsense," Teddy declared, hanging up the phone and rising from his chair. "Kate hasn't arrived yet, either. I was just phoning her apartment, but all I get is her answering machine. Confounded things, I won't talk to them."

"I'm sure she's on her way," Elizabeth said reassuringly.

"You're right. Probably tied up in evening traffic. It's always worse on Fridays. Why don't I fix some drinks? Elizabeth, honey, what'll you have?"

She declined the offer and waited for Giles to order a brandy before saying hello to him. It wasn't the warmest of greetings.

Giles bowed his head. "So she told you," he murmured.

"She didn't have to." Like him, Elizabeth was careful to keep her voice low enough so that her father couldn't hear. "I helped raise Kate, I know when she's hurting."

"If it's any consolation, I'm not proud of what I said the other night."

"It isn't. But I'll admit I am curious to know why you haven't told *her* that."

"I plan to. Do you really believe she's coming?"

Across the room Teddy rattled the ice bucket and grumbled about his secretary pilfering ice cubes for her diet drinks. Observing him, Elizabeth shrugged. "She's a lot like Dad in that she's guided by her emotions. If she's still feeding off her anger, you can count on her being here— and then I'd suggest you prepare yourself to expect the worst. But if she's let the hurt get the best of her . . ." She shook her head. "Personally, I'm not surprised she *isn't* here. She's been spending a great deal of time on that renovation project. Too much. I'm worried she's overdoing it."

"Here we are," Teddy said, joining them and handing Giles his drink. "Who's overdoing what?"

"I was just telling Giles how concerned we are about Kate putting in all those extra hours these days."

Teddy uttered a low growl and brooded into his bourbon. "Used to be you could count on her coming over every night to check on the horses, join us for dinner or at least, dessert—you know Kate and food. This last week or so, I don't think we've seen her more than a minute or two at a time. She's always in a hurry to go somewhere. I'm beginning to regret I ever let her talk me into giving her that building."

Elizabeth laid a hand on the sleeve of his gray suit jacket. "It would break her heart to hear you say that. She's only trying to make you proud of her."

"I'm already proud of her. I'd be even more proud if she'd visit her old man once in a while—and bring a beau!"

"I thought we'd get to that sooner or later," Elizabeth drawled. "Have you tried phoning her office? Maybe she's been held up in a meeting."

Muttering his opinion of slave drivers, Teddy went to try. But it turned out that no one at ABA had seen Kate that afternoon. It was assumed she was still on the renovation site. As he hung up again, Teddy peppered the air with a stream of oaths.

"They *assume*. What kind of operation are they running over there that they don't even have a phone to reach her?"

Giles was barely listening. He had an idea and was debating whether to suggest it or not. "Why don't you two go on to the country club," he finally told them, achieving a casualness he didn't feel. "I can drive across town and see what's keeping her. She's probably just lost track of the time. I'll follow her to her place so she can change and then drive her to the reception."

Teddy grabbed at the idea enthusiastically. "Why that's a fine idea."

"Maybe we should simply wait a few more minutes," Elizabeth said, far less cheerfully. She gave her father a pointed look. "You know how Kate is about surprises."

"Nonsense," Teddy scoffed, avoiding her steady gaze. "She *loves* surprises."

"Dad—"

"Elizabeth. Please." Giles's smile held gentle appeal. "I assure you I'll be—careful."

"Of course you will," Teddy said, all but snatching the glass from Giles's hand and urging him toward the door. "We'll see you there. Don't feel you have to rush."

Leave it to Teddy to grab hold of an idea when it suited him, Giles mused seconds later when the office door was shut behind him and he found himself alone in the hallway. Well, he'd done it now. Wishing he'd had time to gulp down his brandy, he headed for the elevators.

Friday's traffic did seem to be worse than normal and the drive from the Omni building to the renovation site took longer than usual. Yet he barely looked at the dramatic and often ingenious buildings he passed, nor did he pay much more attention to the bevy of smiling, cosmopolitan women who crossed before him whenever he had to stop for a traffic light. His mind was on Kate and what he was going to say when he found her. *If* he found her, he amended dryly. He didn't discount that at this very moment she could be riding up the Omni elevators. The way his luck was going of late, the odds were good.

But when he arrived at the plain but solid-brick building, he found her car still parked in front. He decided to take it as a good omen.

The sounds of electric saws and hammering drifted out through opened windows as he climbed the stairs and let himself in through the front door. Inside, the emptiness amplified the sounds even more. Knowing it would be useless to shout, he wound his way through a maze of rooms, looking for her or someone who could tell him where to find her.

After one false lead and a couple of shrugs, he was back at the stairway ready to try the next floor. A muscle-bound man with sawdust clinging to his sweat-soaked tank top and arms was descending. He answered Giles's inquiry by pointing his hammer toward the ceiling.

"Up one floor with the blueprints."

Giles hesitated, gripping the newly replaced banister. "Is she in conference?"

The man with the Hispanic accent grinned. "Yeah. With the sandman."

Eyeing the man skeptically, but deciding he wasn't going to waste time asking for an explanation, Giles started up the unstained stairs. Whoever this "sandman" was, he told himself, he could postpone the rest of their meeting for another day.

It was the descending sun streaking through a west window that drew him to the room on the left. Dust-filled beams of gold stung his eyes, momentarily blinding him. Squinting and pinching the bridge of his nose, he turned away from the bright light, spotting rolls of foil-wrapped insulation stockpiled like a giant's hoard of cotton candy, and finally the woman who'd apparently fallen asleep while going over a stack of blueprints. Her hair was drawn into a ponytail that streamed out the back of the blue baseball cap. Like long silver-and-gold strands of silk, it tumbled over her shoulder and onto the prints. He didn't have to see her face to know it was Kate; he would recognize that hair anywhere.

For a moment he stood motionless, aware of a warmth spreading inside him, aware that it was the woman and not the closed confines of the room that provoked it. He was amazed that anyone could sleep with all the racket. How exhausted she had to be not to notice. How good it felt to see her again.

He stepped closer, his tentative, bemused smile slowly turning into a frown of concern. Even with her face half-buried in her folded arms, he could see the signs of deep fatigue. Her cheeks were pale and almost gaunt, and there were violet shadows beneath the sable fringe of her eyelashes. Elizabeth was right to be concerned. Like him, Kate had clearly been pushing herself these past two weeks. But on her the effects were disturbing.

The need to talk gave way to the need to provide care. There would be no trip to the country club tonight. She needed to rest. Teddy would understand, or at least Elizabeth would.

"Kate," he murmured, gently stroking his hand over her hair and bringing it to rest on her shoulder. As she roused, he could feel fragile bones and lean muscles shift beneath the soft denim of her workshirt. He experienced a surge of dismay and bitterness. She wasn't built to work like a laborer. Why did she insist on it? What was she trying to prove?

Kate moaned softly and tried to turn away from the voice that called to her. Would he even haunt her dreams? She'd had a few moments of blissful escape. The sun on her back felt so good. If only her mind would stop toying with her for a little while longer. God, even as a beginning rider, even with her worst falls off Zulu, she'd never felt this tired or hurt this badly.

"Come on, Katherine, wake up. You can't stay here."

She sat up with a start. *"You."*

"Me."

She half groaned, half laughed and dropped her head back onto her arms. "This is what I get for telling them to put locks on the front door and not following up on it."

Because he wanted to touch her, brush the dust from her cheek, the violet shadows beneath her eyes, Giles slipped his hands into his pants pockets and tried to keep his tone light. "No need to man the battle stations today, Kate. I'm here under a flag of truce bearing a message of goodwill."

Kate straightened enough to give him an ominous look, trying hard to ignore the charismatic picture he cut standing there in an immaculate camel sports coat, neatly pressed dark brown slacks, white shirt and tie. "I'll consider springing for a bottle of champagne if any of that means you're being deported." When she saw his crooked, indisputably sad smile, she felt her resistance waver and looked away. "No. Well, so much for wishful thinking. What *are* you doing here? I thought you'd said everything there was to say two weeks ago."

"Two weeks ago I might have agreed. But all that can wait for another time. I came to check on you for your father and sister."

"Why would they be—" Kate glanced at her watch and gasped. "The reception!" With a grimace she pushed herself to her feet, wincing as she braced against the table to steady herself. "Tell them I'm on my way. Tell them...I went home to shower and—and change, and I'll be there within the hour."

"You're on your way home all right. But you're going to bed."

Determined to ignore him, she circled the table and began to pass him, aware that in her oversized workshirt and knee-ripped jeans she looked about as threatening as a mouse would be to a lion. Just as she came parallel to him, he stretched out his arm and blocked her path. Kate began to push the arm out of her way, only to cry out and tuck her hands under opposite armpits.

A bitter taste rose to Giles's mouth when he saw how her face contorted with pain. Directly or indirectly, he knew he'd caused this. "Let me see," he muttered.

"Who do you think you are to come here after—*ow!*"

Deciding he felt bad enough without listening to a list of his transgressions, Giles took firm hold of her wrists and jerked so that he could see what she was hiding from him. "Bloody hell," he whispered, seeing the bruises and bloodied blisters that covered both hands. "What have you done to yourself?"

"Hammered nails mostly."

"And a few fingers."

Her only response was a shrug.

"Maybe you wouldn't have done as much damage if you hadn't pretended that each nail was securing the lid on my coffin."

Torn between giggles and tears, she averted her gaze. Tired, she told herself. It wasn't him or his irritating English charm, she was simply bone-deep tired.

"Kate..." He hesitated only a moment before finally giving into the urge to brush away the smudge of dust on her left cheek. "I'll admit you deserve a chance to take your best shot, but couldn't we try a cease-fire instead? Please."

He was so close she could hear his heartbeat—or was that hers? The crisp smell of soap was definitely his; *she* was as grimy as if Zulu had tossed her into a bed of sand. Feeling at a disadvantage and very uncertain, she kept her eyes trained on the paisley silk handkerchief in his breast pocket. "Last time I tried that I was torpedoed broadside, your lordship," she muttered sarcastically.

"Would it help to know that you weren't the only casualty?"

"You needn't say things you think I might want to hear."

"What about things I *need* to say?" When she lifted her eyes, he gave her a crooked smile. "Kate, I think you frighten me."

What was she supposed to say to that—take two aspirin and see a doctor in the morning? She shook her head, a little astonished and growing more confused and nervous by the minute. "I haven't asked for anything but your friendship, Giles. I'm no threat to you."

"You think not?" He looked down at her wrists, aware of his superior strength and that despite it, *he* was the one who felt implacably held. "You've done nothing but amuse, frustrate, intrigue and incite me from the moment we've met. As soon as I think I have you figured out, you do something unexpected to throw me completely off. This for instance," he murmured, rubbing his thumbs in soothing circles. "Kate, it's one thing to take up the battle of the underdog, but don't you think this is going too far?"

"There's so much to do and so little time. It's my fault, really. I'm the one who promised the new tenants they'd be able to move in by the first of October, but I had no idea what was involved. The least I can do is help where I can."

Giles inclined his head. "See what I mean? You're very much one of a kind, my dear, and that's a dangerous thing to be around men who have a reputation for being connoisseurs and cads, albeit charming ones."

Not sure she was following, Kate shook her head. "Are you telling me you did what you did to—protect me from you?" She didn't know whether to laugh or explode. "That's the most ridiculous thing I've ever heard."

"I thought it rather gallant myself."

"Archaic."

"Lord, here we go again. Thank goodness I have no intention of romancing you. You'd drive me to drink before I figured out the right approach."

"You should live so long to get the chance."

"Kate—" With a slight yank he jerked her off balance and against his chest. He hesitated only a moment, to gaze into her dazed, dreamy eyes, to consider her parted lips and acknowledge he was losing more than the battle. "Shut up," he whispered, and pressed his lips to hers.

She'd missed him. She realized it the moment tension found its release. He'd infuriated her, rejected her and had this noble thought of protecting her from himself, but now as she met his searing kiss with equal force, she knew no amount of denial would erase the fact that she'd missed him.

Just a moment longer, Giles told himself as he devoured all she offered and asked for more. Just a moment longer and he would be able to live with the hunger and need. But even as he tried to drag his lips from hers, he found himself taking quick, fierce nips to prolong the moment.

"I guess you showed me," she murmured breathlessly as his mouth grazed her jaw.

"It's been recorded throughout history that Channings have been merciless when the need arose."

She offered him better access to her neck. "You've certainly got me shaking in my sneakers."

"That's fatigue." And *that* reminded him that he needed to stop before he couldn't. He placed her at arm's length and gave her cap a playful tug. "Come on. I'll take you home."

Miffed that he could recover so much more quickly than she, Kate pushed her cap up off her nose and pertly announced, "I can take myself home, thank you."

"You're dead on your feet. If you get behind the wheel of a car, you're liable to pass out and run over some poor woman walking her poodle. Besides, those hands need tending." When she began to protest he raised his hands to silence her. "All right. At least let me follow you."

The warmth of his kiss still lingered on her lips. It coaxed her into agreeing.

In the end she was grateful for his attentiveness. At a red traffic light, basking in the warm sunlight, she would have dozed off if it weren't for Giles behind her, lightly tapping his horn. Had she been alone, the police could have been called, a wrecker truck could have hauled her off and she would have slept through the whole thing.

Giles pointed that out as he placed a hand at the small of her back and urged her up the stairs to her apartment. "And you ran two yellow lights," he added, shifting his arm around her waist when she stumbled.

"Maybe, but think of all the poodles in town who'll live to see another day." She didn't quite succeed in stifling a yawn.

"Where are your keys?" When she handed them over, he shook his head. "Those are car keys."

She remembered that she'd sent her car for an oil change earlier and had taken her other keys off the ring. When her car had been returned, she'd dropped them into her shirt pocket where they would be easy for her to reach. Now as she tried to get the others from her back pocket, she found that process far more painful.

With a sigh, she bumped one hip toward him. "Could you help?"

"Only you could get yourself into this kind of predicament." He leaned close and slid his hand deep into the pocket that followed the subtle roundness of her bottom. As she turned her head slightly, their breaths mingled, their eyes clung. "What would you have done if I were a stranger?"

The words floated dizzily in her head. But despite her weariness, a hint of laughter bubbled to her lips and she impishly kissed his chin. "I'd have suggested you introduce yourself, of course."

Feeling like a man about to walk a very short plank, Giles drew out the keys and unlocked her apartment door. It was cool and dark inside. Kate had forgotten to open the drapes as she usually did before leaving for work.

She went straight to her bedroom, where she slid off her cap and tossed it in the direction of a chair. "I should call Daddy and Elizabeth, shouldn't I?" she asked, dropping onto her bed and moaning with pleasure.

Did she have eyes in the back of her head, or had she simply assumed he would follow? Giles pushed away from the doorjamb and slid out of his jacket. "I'll do it after I see to your hands. Why don't you undress and get into bed while I hunt everything down?"

"I need a shower."

"It can wait until morning."

"My alarm...I have to set my alarm."

"For what? Tomorrow's Saturday, for heaven's sake. It won't kill you to take a day off."

She struggled to reach over and turn the knob anyway. "I have to compete tomorrow. The charity horse show."

Giles swore under his breath. "Of all the stubborn females—"

"It has nothing to do with stubbornness. There's a thousand-dollar check that's awarded to the winner's favorite charity. For three years now I've donated mine to the children's hospital's cancer rehabilitation program.''

"And I'm telling you you're not going to be in any shape to wrestle with that black devil tomorrow. Just cut your losses and try to get some sleep. I'll take care of the rest.''

Kate began to sit up and ended up half leaning against him. "Just because we're speaking again doesn't mean you can boss me around. I don't like bossy men,'' she declared, focusing on his mouth.

Giles pulled the elastic band from her hair as carefully as he could. Tossing it on the bed stand, he combed his fingers through her hair, trying not to think about how much he enjoyed the small task. "Well, I don't like argumentative women. So what do you propose we do about it?''

She brushed her lips ever so lightly against his. "Find a common ground on which to—communicate.''

"Mmm. What if you don't remember this conversation when you're in better shape to—ah—communicate?''

"I'm counting on you to remind me.''

As she lost her battle with fatigue and let her head roll against his shoulder, Giles wasn't sure if he was more disappointed or relieved. But accepting that he wasn't quite ready to release her, he drew her completely into his arms and began to rock her gently.

"Sweet, sweet Kate,'' he whispered, feeling her succumb to the pull of sleep. He brushed his lips against her warm forehead. "Here's another fine mess we've gotten ourselves into.''

Seven

———

It was the pain that woke her. The same needlelike pricks and aching spasms that had interrupted her sleep throughout the night. The same pain that had snatched her out of wonderful dreams. It centered in her hands, though the soreness that stiffened the rest of her body wasn't much better. Moaning, she rolled onto her stomach and lifted her heavy eyelids to view the damage.

Gauze. She looked like a prizefighter before he slipped on his boxing gloves. No, *after* a fight, she amended, wincing as she flexed her fingers and felt the resistance and sting. The only thing that made the hurt bearable was seeing the bandages and recalling—well, vaguely—how Giles had performed first aid on her last night.

He'd been so attentive. So *funny* she thought, slowly smiling as she remembered the limericks he'd begun to re-cite when the pain had wakened her. And tender, she concluded, her smile softening as she thought of the way he'd lifted her onto his lap to—

Startled out of her daydreaming, she shifted slightly to look down and saw that she still wore her ice-blue camisole and tap pants. Relieved, she exhaled in a swoosh and buried her face into her pillow. Well, well...when the man took control, he took control.

She closed her eyes and relived the kiss they'd shared earlier. It had been the best medicine of all.

Where was he now?

He would be back.

He wanted her.

The thought made her smile into her pillow. He might not like the idea—she was still a bit shaky about it herself—but there was no sense denying it at this point. They'd tried their best and neither of them could make the attraction go away.

It didn't resolve anything. Not one thing. Yet, somehow that suited her, too.

Following the straight and narrow had never been her style. She enjoyed the thrill of experiencing the unknown. She had no fear of climbing onto Zulu's back or of facing a steeplechase course. Maybe she should just approach this thing with Giles the same way. Maybe if they had an affair after all, they could get it out of their systems and get on with their lives.

"Lunatic," she sighed, and with a groan she pushed herself up by her elbows. First things first. She needed a shower, aspirin and lots of coffee. This was going to be a full day, and if she planned to even attempt to think clearly—

Her gaze froze on the position of the alarm switch, the clock radio and then shifted to the time. As a silent *uh-oh* formed in her mind, she shifted to consider the bright sunshine filtering in through the closed slats of her mini-blinds. Her mouth dropped open to gasp or scream, she wasn't sure which.

He wouldn't.

He did.

He'd switched off her alarm.

Anguish and indignation swelled inside her like a bubbling spring. How could he? How *dare* he? Hadn't she explained what this competition meant to her?

She scissor kicked her way free of the bedsheet and swung her legs to the floor. Dizziness dulled the pain, but not the panic. She had two hours to pull herself together, to get to Meadowbrook and to trailer Zulu back to Atlanta. Unless she sprouted wings or got some help she would never make it.

"Oh, that man," she ground out between her clenched teeth. Give him an inch and he'd taken a foot!

Reaching for the phone, she tried to punch the number of Meadowbrook's foreman. But the way her hands were bandaged, her fingers were bound together and she kept hitting two digits at once.

With a sound of impatience, she hung up and, lifting her hand to her mouth, yanked off the adhesive strip securing the gauze with her teeth. Then, circling her head in one direction and her hand in the opposite, she managed to unwind the three feet of gauze.

Her stomach rolled at the sight of what she'd done to herself. Yesterday she hadn't really had the time or inclination to look. No wonder Giles had spent so much time fussing with her. Of course, it looked worse than it felt. Almost.

Could she blame him for being concerned? Could she be angry with him for doing what he'd believed was right?

Before yesterday, the answer would have come without hesitation. Now, she nibbled on her lower lip and mused over the changes twenty-four hours could bring.

The old Kate would have wanted to strangle him. At the least she would have wanted to give him a good piece of her mind for interfering. She'd fought too hard to earn her independence from her family to tolerate anyone meddling in her life, and she still felt that way.

More or less.

"Oh, that man." This time her voice was a low murmur, and a resigned smile curved her lips. She reached for the phone again.

"Jackson," she said, upon hearing the familiar and worried voice of Meadowbrook's foreman. "Yes, I know I was supposed to be there twenty minutes ago. That's why I'm calling. I've had a small problem and I'm going to need your help."

Giles couldn't believe she'd outmaneuvered him. Even fifteen minutes ago as he'd stood outside her apartment door knocking and knocking, he couldn't believe she would awake in time, let alone be in any condition to compete. Only after he'd thought to look below and saw that her car was gone, did it hit him.

With the bouquet he'd brought as a peace offering in one hand and the gauze and medicated cream a pharmacist had recommended for her hands in the other, he'd stood there feeling like a fool. Whatever confidence he'd had about having done the right thing in his attempt to let her get the rest she needed vanished like the bill he'd handed the vendor for the fresh cut flowers. All he could do was visualize her reaction when she woke up this morning and discovered he'd ignored her explanation about the charity horse show and intentionally shut off her alarm.

Blast it all, but she had moxie. Moxie, hell. The woman was resolute. What should he have done, tied her to her bed?

And now what? he brooded. He supposed it wouldn't hurt to go make sure she'd arrived at the arena safely, not that he had any great urge to watch her play masochist. But then he considered his options . . . like going to the health club he'd joined and doing some laps in the pool . . . *a lot of laps if he intended to push Kate completely out of his mind* . . . writing home . . . *and lying about how terrific his life was* . . . calling O'Keefe . . . *and letting him laugh himself sick over the mess he'd gotten himself into*— It was all he needed to urge him back to the Jaguar, toss in the bouquet and the bag with the medication and drive back downtown.

She was going to be in a wax, but maybe he could calm her down somewhat before she rode. He didn't want her annoyance with him jeopardizing her safety. Life was becoming complicated enough without adding guilt to it.

He arrived to find the covered arena filling rapidly and, after finding the Beaumonts' reserved ringside box empty, circled to the stables. There he found women in silk and men in suits mingling with hay and horses as well-wishers circled friends or relatives competing in the show.

He was about to ask directions to the Beaumont stall when he heard a familiar, angry neigh from outside the stables. A number of conversations suddenly stopped in midsentence, a few horses shifted nervously and more than a few people wondered aloud at the wisdom in riding an animal with that temperament. Silently agreeing, Giles followed the sound outside to the loading and unloading area.

He spotted the Meadowbrook truck and trailer immediately, parked slightly away from everyone else. Teddy
and Elizabeth watched as Kate and a wiry man he recognized as Jackson, the foreman, worked on grooming the
stallion who clearly would have preferred being back at
Meadowbrook chasing the wind. Teddy, in a white suit and
Panama hat, watched proudly. Elizabeth was lovely as ever
in a black, wide-brimmed straw hat and a matching coat-
dress, but Giles found his gaze riveted on Kate.

He'd never seen her in a formal riding habit before and
decided the elegant, tailored lines suited her lithe figure as
much as the black coat emphasized her fair coloring.
When she turned toward him, sunlight glistened off her
highly-polished black boots and the simple gold pin on her
white stock. But that wasn't what made him blink. It was
the bright, welcoming smile she gave him when she spotted him.

"You made it! I'm so glad."

She extended a gloved hand to him. Like a sleepwalker
he stepped forward to take it. Gently. He raised it to his
lips, aware of the padding he could feel beneath the thin
leather. Bandages. It explained why she was wearing them
when regulations allowed riders to go gloveless in warm
weather. He glanced up to find her watching him, a touch
of amusement in her eyes, as well as wariness. He lifted an
eyebrow in question. If anyone should be wary...

"I was afraid I would be intruding."

"Nonsense," Teddy declared as if the comment had
been directed at him. "Didn't I tell you last night when you
phoned that you were welcome to join us?"

Giles kept his eyes on Kate. "Am I welcome?"

Her breath locked in her throat. A shiver of excitement
raced through her body. In his navy blazer and pleated
white slacks he looked as dashing as a yachtsman about to

board a clipper and sail off to Bermuda. She'd believed she was immune to such flamboyance, but her heartbeat told her otherwise.

"A knight errant should witness the fruit of his labors."

Elizabeth coughed discreetly and took hold of her father's arm. "Dad, I'm about to melt in this sun. Besides, I think it's time we took our seats. We'll see you later, Katherine, dear. Best of luck."

Teddy blew Kate a kiss and allowed himself to be led off, but not entirely without complaint. "Couldn't you have waited another few seconds? Things were just getting interesting."

Watching them leave, Kate chuckled and then turned back to Giles, only to discover that though he'd released her hand, he'd moved closer. Hardly aware of Jackson, who stood on the other side of Zulu talking soothingly as he brushed the horse, she lifted her head and peered under the brim of her black riding hat to meet Giles's unsettling scrutiny.

"I suppose you'll lecture now?" she murmured demurely.

"Give me a moment to recover from the shock."

She didn't pretend to misunderstand and her smile was quick and pleased. "You expected a tongue lashing, did you?"

"At the least a bruised shin."

"It was going to be death by strangulation."

"I don't suppose you'd have done it with Othello's style and added a kiss?"

Kate fingered his navy- and red-striped tie. "Not very original."

"Well, I'd be open to suggestions, of course." When she laughed, the sound went through him like a summer wind whipping around a city building, warm yet stunning. He found himself inching closer to her until Jackson began to hum under his breath, reminding him of where they were. Giles sighed. "What's going on, Kate?"

She drew her lips into a pout. "It isn't considered good form to point out to a lady that you're aware she's trying to turn over a new leaf."

"I'm not sure I want any leaves turned. You're near impossible to resist as it is."

Pleasure made her eyes shimmer like precious stones. "Can I remind you that you said that the next time you're infuriated with me?"

"Kate, about last night—"

With an impatient sound, Jackson tossed his brush into the back of the trailer and announced, "I'm going to go get a drink of water to wash down the dust."

Kate watched him stomp away. "Poor Jackson," she murmured. "I think we've embarrassed him. Go on, Giles. What about last night?"

How could she be so calm? He felt as tense and troubled as if he were about to make a life or death decision—and perhaps he was. "I don't want to hurt you."

"That's nice. I've decided I don't want to hurt you, either."

"But I will if this goes any further."

Zulu seemed to pick up on something in Giles's voice and whinnied, nudging Kate in the shoulder as if to urge her away. She stroked him absently, but kept her gaze on Giles.

"Do you always feel compelled to warn away women you want to take to bed?"

"Kate, if it were a simple matter of taking you to bed, we'd have already been there."

She had to look away and concentrated a moment on the watchful horse beside her. "Do you know that noble streak in you annoyed me in the beginning. Maybe I knew even then that it would come down to this. I'd half hoped you might simply seduce me and I wouldn't have to worry that I wanted you more than is healthy. Now you're demanding I make a conscious decision and when I do, you'll know how vulnerable I am to you."

The need to touch was irresistible and Giles reached out to stroke her cheek with the back of his fingers. "Don't you think I already see that? That's what makes this so bloody complicated. I want you, Kate. It's a good thing we're not alone right now or I'd be tempted to show you how much. I want to learn everything there is to know about your sleek little body and what it takes to make you come apart in my arms...what it sounds like...what it feels like. Damn it, I ache just thinking of how it would be between us."

His voice, deeper than usual, seeped into her like warm honey. Already light-headed from the sun and mesmerized by the green fire heating his eyes, she felt the world around her spin and had to close her eyes and rest a hand against his chest to steady herself.

"Kate?"

"I'm sorry, it's only—"

Giles swore and slid an arm around her, drawing her closer. "I should be horsewhipped for doing this to you now of all times."

"It's only the heat and the aspirin on an empty stomach. I get this reaction sometimes."

His comment to that was succinct. He glanced over at Zulu, who looked more energetic and restless than ever. "Kate, don't ride today. You're in no condition to wrestle with him. Surely your father's told you the same thing?"

"He doesn't know." Kate shook off the weak feeling and looked up to see his grim-faced reaction. She reached up to smooth away one of the deepening grooves framing his beautiful mouth. "Giles Channing, don't you even *think* of telling him."

"He's not blind. He can see what's beneath that skillful application of makeup."

"I thought you said I was irresistible?" As he narrowed his eyes and began to reply, she shifted her finger to cover his lips. "No, don't scold. Even if Daddy knew, he'd understand why I need to compete today. I told you before—I'm not doing this because of ego, Giles. There are people counting on me."

"Hell, *I'll* write the rehabilitation center a check!"

"That would be lovely. I'm sure they'll appreciate it. But you still don't understand. The press this receives helps remind others of the program's existence and their many needs. It's one of the few times a year that I don't mind talking to reporters. Now why don't you kiss me for good luck and go take your seat. As you can see, you're making Zulu edgy, and I need to calm him down before we go in for our practice run."

Giles didn't much care for being so neatly dismissed and was tempted to argue. What disturbed him more was recognizing the impulse he had to pick her up and carry her off to his car. But he could see by the determined lift of her chin and her steady gaze that she wouldn't easily forgive him if he did.

Feeling like he was being ripped in two, he cupped her face within his hands and lowered his head. "By God you stay in that saddle and come out of this in one piece," he whispered against her lips.

"Will you be waiting?" she challenged, drawing confidence from the passion she saw in his eyes.

"What choice do I have?"

His kiss took her breath away. She'd expected punishment; his impatience and frustration simmered so near the surface, he was flushed from it. But instead he took her mouth with a gentleness, an entreaty that wrenched a breathless moan from her. Wrapped in the cocoon of his embrace, tantalized by the caress of his lips and tongue, he laid silent claim to her heart.

Giles could feel it, knew he'd asked for more than he'd consciously meant to; but her response was so generous, so complete that he was unable to do anything but bask in the pleasure of it. Yet she made him crave more, much more. Things, emotions that had no name but fostered a hunger inside him he hadn't known existed.

He was a gambler at heart, but not necessarily an adventurer, yet she tempted him to risk everything on a visceral something that he wasn't even sure he understood. The magnitude of it rocked him. With a muttered oath, he forced himself away from her and strode back toward the arena.

Dazed, Kate watched him go until someone cleared his throat behind her. She turned to see Jackson peering at her from under Zulu's neck. She hadn't even been aware he'd returned.

"Now do you think you could get your mind back on business?" he grumbled.

He was right of course, she thought, casting him a sheepish look. This was no time to be dwelling on her increasingly complicated private life, but she couldn't help teasing him a little. "Jackson, you have no sense of romance."

"It ain't romance that'll keep you on this demon's back over those jumps, missy."

"I'll stay on him. Let's just hope he's in the mood to behave during dressage." She stroked Zulu's strong neck to allow Jackson time to get him saddled. Though the horse tolerated the little man more than most, both were wary of each other.

When Kate accepted a lift up, the stallion's ears flicked back and forth, his powerful muscles bunched slightly beneath the saddle. But then he relaxed and stood steady. "That's my boy," she murmured, giving his neck one final stroke. Finally, with the lightest pressure in her hands and knees, she turned him and followed Jackson toward the ring.

"Well, it could be worse," Teddy drawled philosophically as the final dressage scores were posted and he compared them to the penned notes in his program. "She's sure to pull up in the jumping event."

Elizabeth fanned herself with her own program. "No doubt, but how much? She's never had to do it from third place before, and that second-place horse from Wildwood Stables is going to be hard to beat, too. I didn't know Lester Northcutt's stables could produce a horse of that caliber."

"I heard he'd been thinking about selling out to some Kentucky investor. Maybe the deal went through."

Elizabeth paused to give her father a gently reproachful look. "Do you mean to say that we could have new neighbors and you didn't tell me?"

"Well, it's not like you're going to bake a pie and walk through the rose garden to deliver it," Teddy grumbled. "Besides I'm not certain that old Lester *did* sell." He leaned forward and gave Giles an innocent smile. "You know that's a prime piece of property adjoining ours. Not as large as Meadowbrook, you understand, but if a shrewd

investor had a notion to clear out half of those confounded woods and hire himself a first-class foreman, he'd
have a nice start, yessir.''

"Father, you're about as subtle as a robin standing over
a worm hole.''

While Teddy snorted and sat back in his seat to exchange words with the couple in the next box, Giles indulged in a low laugh and reached over to give Elizabeth's
hand a squeeze. "It's all right," he assured her. "Your father and I have an understanding—he's allowed to drop all
the hints he wants and I'm allowed to pretend that he's
talking to someone behind me.''

"Would that extend to me if I brought up the subject of
my sister?''

Giles thought of the way Elizabeth had handled her father so that he and Kate could have a few minutes alone,
how she'd silently offered him her handkerchief to wipe off
Kate's lipstick, and he decided she deserved some kind of
reassurance. "We got off to a shaky start last night," he
admitted, quietly. "But she's decided to forgive me, at
least momentarily.''

Elizabeth ducked her head to hide a smile. "I think you
could understand her very well. Still, what I wanted to talk
about was her health. Doesn't she appear...fragile to
you?''

He thought about the kind of work Kate had been exposing herself to, the resulting injury to her hands and her
desire to keep it a secret. "Always. Despite her feisty temperament.''

"But more so now.''

"She's been working exceptionally hard, Elizabeth.''

"I suppose what I'm asking is, will you try to see that
she slows down?''

It might be easier to harness the wind. He also wondered how wise it would be for him to become so involved with her. "I can try," he murmured as the first horse and rider entered the arena for the jumping competition.

One by one the contestants took their turn. The spectators, graciously supportive, cheered on successes and sympathized with the failures. Giles applauded politely for the better performances, but with every strong showing he grew more and more tense about the competition that was lining up against Kate. It didn't help that she'd pulled the last slot. He knew it wouldn't work well for Zulu. Having had a taste of the ring, the stallion would be impatient to get out there again and burn off some of his enormous energy. And it would be doubly hard on Kate, whose questionable reserve of energy would be draining fast in this heat.

To add to his concern, a commotion broke out in the stables between rides and a horse's furious scream could be heard throughout the arena. Giles and the Beaumonts exchanged looks. There was no mistaking which horse it came from, they only wondered what had happened to set him off this time, as well as about the results of his temper. Within seconds Giles was half out of his seat to go investigate, but Teddy convinced him that the people best able to get things under control were already there.

Things did settle down, but by the time the stallion from Wildwood entered the ring, Giles's spine was rigid with tension. The good news was that the first-place horse had disappointed the crowd with a mediocre showing. The bad news was the stallion, slightly smaller than Zulu but no less flashy, now had the lead and appeared eager to keep it.

Perhaps too eager, Giles realized a few minutes later. The rider let the horse have too much control and raced the jumps. As a result, his two knockdowns cost him what otherwise would have been a formidable lead.

"She needs a perfect ride. But if anyone can do it, she can," Teddy said, voicing everyone's thoughts as Kate's turn was announced. "Show 'em how it's done, Katy!"

"Dad," Elizabeth scolded in a loud whisper. "This isn't a rodeo."

"A man has a right to cheer on his own flesh and blood, doesn't he?"

Giles did his cheering silently, his gaze locked on woman and horse as if he could will them on to success. What was she feeling? he wondered, trying to gauge her thoughts by her expression. It was hopeless. The professional in her had slipped on a mask of cool composure. She could be scared out of her wits and only she and Zulu would know it. But he did eye the deepening patches of feverish pink on her cheeks with mounting concern. Obviously the aspirin were wearing off. The question was, could she hold on a little longer?

The course, unlike those he was used to seeing in Europe, was tight, the fences seemingly one on top of the other. Because of his great size, it appeared Zulu was at a disadvantage, yet from the first jump Kate had him reaching for the fence and sailing over in a clean arc as if they'd been practicing in this particular ring for weeks. In and out they weaved, taking the great wall with a grace that drew appreciative gasps from the crowd.

Hold on, Giles willed silently as Kate directed the stallion toward the final triple combination. The arena seemed to pulsate with the sound of working hoofs and lungs. Two short jumps and a neck-breaking third where timing was everything. Zulu went into it with the eagerness of a champion. When they flew over the final fence, Giles felt his heart leap with them. Doing everything in her power to help him, Kate rose off Zulu's back and leaned low over his neck. Only by watching the rigidity of her jaw could Giles see her sudden spasm of pain as the stallion landed hard but cleanly.

A roar of cheers and applause filled the arena. Giles clapped automatically, but his mind was on Kate's expression as they landed. The bandages under her glove should have offered suitable protection. What had happened?

"She won! Oh, isn't it wonderful, she won!" Elizabeth cried, applauding even more enthusiastically. "Let's go congratulate her."

Giles didn't need a second invitation. He was half out of his seat when Teddy insisted they wait for her to accept her award first.

"How sweet," Elizabeth said, touching her fingertips to her lips as, minutes later, Kate rode out to accept her award. "She's about to cry. Why, she's never cried before."

It wasn't because of winning. Giles knew it the moment he saw her brush an escaping tear from one eye. Deciding he couldn't wait any longer, he rose and, excusing himself, headed straight for the stables.

Kate was grateful that Jackson met her at the gate. Despite Zulu's protest, he took hold of the horse's reins and led him through the crowded stables, outside to the trailer.

"Congratulations, Kate."

She'd been dismounting and the sound of the gravelly voice behind her almost made her lose her balance. Strong hands gripped her waist and, as she turned, she discovered that her ears weren't playing tricks on her after all.

"Morgan!" she gasped and threw her arms around the powerfully built man's neck for a spontaneous hug. "Oh, Morgan, what a wonderful surprise."

"Hello, brat. You did well."

"Well? We were terrific."

He gave her a lopsided smile. "Good enough to beat my horse. Dancer's Prize," he explained seeing the confusion in her eyes.

"Dancer's Prize is yours? But I thought he belonged to Wildwood Stables?"

"He does."

It took her a moment, but she finally picked up on what he was saying. "You? You're working at Wildwood?"

"I own the place."

She realized it was true the moment she recognized the quality of his natural-colored sports coat and gray slacks. "Why that's *wonderful*, that's—wait a minute. Then it was your rider's stupidity that nearly got me knocked off my horse."

"I just heard. That's part of the reason I came over. I wanted to be sure you were all right. Believe me, it won't happen again."

Realizing that he meant to fire the young man, Kate grimaced and shrugged. "Forget it. I was able to calm Zulu down and things worked out well. Let me look at you."

She leaned back to study him, her eyes twinkling with pleasure and amusement. Between the ages of ten and fifteen she'd believed Morgan Deveroux was the sexiest, most handsome man she'd ever laid eyes on. He was still extremely attractive in a dark, roguish sort of way, but her crush had settled into warm affection—and deep respect. No one had ever challenged her to excel as Morgan had, and no one had been a better friend while doing it.

"Ten years," she murmured, considering the wavy black hair he still wore in a style that just brushed against his collar, the squared features and onyx eyes that could impale like a lance when his temper got the best of him—as it often did. "You look better then ever."

"You look beat."

"Still determined to insult your way into everyone's heart, I see." Laughing, she hugged him again. "I'm so glad you're back. And you're staying?"

"Oh, yes. I'm staying. Though somehow I doubt the rest of your family will be as pleased with the news as you are."

"Daddy might grumble a bit about your abrupt departure. Anyway, you know how he likes to think no one can do anything or get anywhere without his help."

"I heard about Daniel Kirkland. How's Elizabeth?"

"You know Liz. She puts on a good front and keeps her true feelings inside. Still, she's avoided getting in a plane since the crash. They should be here in a moment. Would you like to say hello?"

"Maybe some other time."

Kate watched something hard come and go in his eyes and impulsively reached up to kiss his cheek. "I hope you'll make it soon. I missed you, Morgan. And I don't care what you say, I don't think I was the only one at Meadowbrook who did."

He began to respond but stopped when he looked over her shoulder. "I was about to ask if there'd been any big changes in your life," he drawled. "But I think I have my answer. Take a look behind you and tell me if that's not the face of a man who wishes he were carrying a set of dueling pistols under his arm?"

Eight

He'd never pictured himself as a jealous man. He'd never had anything, anyone who'd inspired the feeling in him, not women, property or money. In fact he'd given away enough money in his time to consider himself generous. But the emotions Giles experienced as he exited the stables to find Kate in the arms of a stranger covered a lot of territory, none of which came close to resembling generosity. Maybe it would have been easier if the man had been just any man, but it didn't take more than a look to tell he wasn't.

He was slightly over average height, but his strong build gave the impression that he was stockier; a man who'd seen hard times and was used to working with his hands. If his clothes were anything to go by, the work had paid off. *Driven*, was the word that came to mind as Giles studied the man's dark features. And not necessarily at peace yet. An intriguing individual, he concluded; however, what disturbed him most was seeing that Kate obviously thought so, too.

"Hello," she said, greeting him. Giles noted that as tired as she looked, she was amused, too, and a little wary. "Come meet a friend."

No doubt someone had once said that about Benedict Arnold, as well, Giles thought, stepping closer. However, as uncharitable as his inner feelings were, etiquette demanded he extend his right hand. At the same time, he couldn't resist slipping his left arm around Kate's waist and drawing her snugly to his side. He assured himself it was for support because she looked so tired.

As Kate went through the introductions, Giles met Morgan's sardonic smile with an appraising one of his own. "So you're the investor from Kentucky I've been hearing about," he drawled. "Teddy was just telling me that Wildwood is a prime piece of real estate...and so well located."

"That was part of the attraction."

"Undoubtedly."

"But not in the way you think."

"I can't tell you how relieved I am to hear that."

Kate glanced from one man to the other, not sure what was going on but convinced she didn't like it. "Would someone like to know what *I* think?" she asked with feigned sweetness. "Or should I go have a pedicure while you two stand there beating your chests?"

Morgan laughed briefly. "She never did have a very long fuse," he told Giles. "Except when it came to working with horses. Speaking of which—I have a mare that I'd like to introduce to your Zulu, Kate. Interested?"

"After that crack?"

"Going to make me grovel, eh?"

"I'd have more luck getting Liz on a horse." But the mention of her sister gave her an idea and her eyes brightened with a mischievous gleam. "Of course, I would be willing to listen to an offer—provided you'd be willing to come to Meadowbrook for dinner sometime."

"They might not thank you for that."

There were secrets in his eyes that Kate couldn't read, but she did pick up on his interest and decided to play out her hand. "Chicken?"

A gust of wind blew about them, hot and dry, but no drier than Morgan's laugh. He reached into his pocket for his billfold and drew out a card. "Call me. Just remember when it all hits the fan, you were an accessory."

Kate wanted to talk to him more, find out what he'd been doing these past ten years, watch Elizabeth's reaction when she saw him; but someone came with a message. After giving her a quick kiss and exchanging handshakes with Giles, Morgan excused himself and left.

Giles watched as Kate bemusedly studied the business card before tucking it into her pocket. "I'll probably regret asking this, but what was that all about?"

"You're quick to jump to conclusions—haven't you figured it all out? Maybe I'm planning an assignation with the man."

"Amusing."

"No more or *less* than you're being." She slipped off her hat, pulled out a few pins and shook her hair free. "Actually, I was just playing a hunch about chemistry. You see, there used to be a lot of it between Morgan and Elizabeth."

Giles lifted both eyebrows. "I don't believe it," he muttered, glancing around only to discover the man was either lost in the crowd or had vanished into thin air. "Good God, Kate. The man's a renegade."

"He is not! He may be tough, but he's also kind."

"He has the eyes of a cobra."

"I always thought they were rather sexy myself."

Narrowing his eyes, Giles gave her a slight jerk, bringing her body completely against his. "That makes twice in the last ten minutes that you've reduced me to feeling base emotions, my dear."

"So I've noticed."

"Try to hold off looking smug until I get used to—damn." He closed his eyes briefly. "With all this going on I forgot to congratulate you."

"He remembers," she sighed, gazing up to the sky. Then she dropped her gaze to his mouth and wet her lips. "Are you going to do it properly?"

How he wanted to. But he didn't even have to look to be aware of the growing number of people around, and neither he nor Kate needed that kind of press to show up in tomorrow's papers. Besides that, he could see that Kate was functioning on sheer bravado. He needed to get her out of this heat to someplace where she could lie down before she collapsed.

"Do it now," she urged. "Quickly before the others come."

Unable to resist, he lowered his head and brushed his lips against hers with a gentleness that belied the frustration of his feelings. "You were magnificent. Wonderful. Superb." With every word he bestowed another feather-light kiss, until he heard her soft whimper. Smiling, he raised his head. But the smile vanished the moment he saw the dazed look on her face.

"Please don't start with the I told you so's," she said, before he could speak. "Just promise me that you won't let me fall flat on my face in front of all these people and totally humiliate myself."

"A condition that can be remedied easily enough," he muttered, swinging her into his arms.

"Giles, that isn't necessary." Kate didn't have a chance to say more before the world went into a spin. With a weak moan she laid her head on his shoulder. No sooner did she close her eyes than she heard her father's bellowing voice.

"Kate! Channing, what's happened?" Teddy hurried to join them with Elizabeth right behind him.

Giles glanced down, catching Kate's wince, and asked with gruff tenderness, "Do you want to tell him or should I?"

"What I'd like is to get out of here before we create an even bigger scene."

"Milady's wish is my command," he murmured for her ears alone before lifting his gaze to Teddy. "She didn't want to worry you before, but she's not feeling well. Shall we get her to her apartment?" He looked to where Jackson was loading Zulu into the trailer. "I'll take her in my car, but we need someone to drive hers."

"We'll do it," Elizabeth replied. "Dad you can have Clarence follow us in the limousine. All I need is her keys."

The arrangements made and keys exchanged, Giles carried Kate to the Jaguar. Kate knew they were attracting attention, could hear the whirring sound of cameras clicking, and she kept her eyes closed. But even knowing they might both live to regret this scene, she couldn't deny it felt wonderful.

"I can feel your heart hammering," she murmured without opening her eyes. "Are you sure I'm not too heavy?"

How could he tell her that she'd all but scared him out of five years of his life or that even with that concern, it thrilled him to be able to hold her? The emotions were all new and more than a little terrifying.

"Don't be absurd," he muttered. "I've swatted at flies that weigh more than you. When was the last time you ate a decent meal?"

"I don't know. I've been busy. Do you want to take me out for another beer and hot dog?"

"Would you kindly not remind me of that night? I think that's where all my troubles began."

She smiled vaguely. "Uh-uh. Your troubles began the night we met when you followed me down to the stables. Mine, too, for that matter—but women are far more pragmatic about these things than men."

"Do tell."

"Really," she insisted, despite her tongue feeling heavy in her mouth. She swallowed, wishing for a cool drink of anything. "Maybe I wasn't any less thrilled with the attraction than you were, but once I realized it wasn't going to go away, I accepted it."

"Malarkey."

"I beg your pardon?"

They'd reached his car and Giles set Kate on her feet so he could get his keys. "Piffle...baloney...tommyrot!"

"Oh, I get it. This is like *Jeopardy!*, right? Now let me see...I need the proper question. How about, 'What are British board games?'"

Having unlocked the door, Giles yanked it open. "Kate, you fought it tooth and nail just as I had until... until..." Remembering the night at the theater, the annoyance seeped out of him in a weary sigh.

"I'll accept a kiss as reparation," she murmured, reaching up to brush a lock of his hair off his forehead.

With something closer to a laugh than a growl, he leaned close and cupped his hand around her face. "By God, I've never considered muzzling a woman before, but you tempt me. Now get in."

Wrinkling her nose at him, she did. The heat inside the car was stifling and she immediately reached for the pin securing her stock. By the time Giles climbed in on the driver's side, her soliloquy had degenerated to little more than caustic grumbling because her gloves made the simple task impossible.

"Let me." He gently brushed her hands away and removed the pin. After slipping it into her coat pocket, he removed the stock and opened the first two buttons on her blouse. Pausing only to turn the ignition key so that the air-conditioning could start, he then helped her out of her jacket. "The gloves, too?"

"I'd rather not look until I have to."

Giles thought about the spasm of pain she'd fought to control on that last jump and Zulu's shriek earlier, and he drew in a deep breath to keep himself from indulging in his own string of oaths. "What happened before you came out in the ring? We heard Zulu, so don't try to deny something did."

"One of the other riders foolishly took hold of his reins. You know how Zulu feels about strangers, particularly men. He reared and I had to fight to hold on and calm him down. In the process I hit my left hand against a stall."

This time Giles did swear and grimly wrenched the shift stick into gear. "That does it—as soon as I get you home, I'm calling a doctor."

Though Kate protested, insisting that she only needed a good night's sleep, once they arrived at her apartment and her father and sister joined them, she found herself outnumbered. Giving up, she let Elizabeth lead her to her bedroom. She knew better than to hope the doctor wouldn't make a house call. Dr. Quisenberry had been the family physician who'd brought her into the world. If he knew she needed medical attention, he would have flown to the North Pole. Twenty minutes after her father phoned, the doctor was knocking on the door, polite but somber.

He exited nearly an hour later in a far more jovial mood.

"What a character," he chuckled, waving away the offer to join Giles and Teddy in a glass of brandy. "You know she was reciting limericks to me the whole time I was rebandaging her hands? There's one about a surgeon from Leeds...poor Elizabeth's coloring hasn't returned to normal yet. I hope I can remember how it goes so I can tell Emily when I—"

"Doctor," Giles interrupted quickly. "Uh, what about her condition?"

"Oh, yes. Well, I don't know how you're going to get her to behave, but she needs to kick back for a few days, regain her strength and let those hands heal. I gave her a sedative to help her sleep through the initial pain and I'll call the pharmacy and have some antibiotics sent over."

"I'll see that she gets her rest," Teddy grumbled into his brandy as Dr. Quisenberry closed the door behind himself. "I'll have her thrown off the job, threaten to remove my funding for the project if that's what it'll take."

Giles shook his head. "Knowing Kate, she'd haul you to court for breach of contract."

"Do you have a better idea?"

"No. Yes. I don't know. Let me sleep on it." He caught Teddy's curious look and smoothed a hand over his hair, feeling more awkward by the minute. "She—ah—mentioned that she'd made a promise to the new tenants, something about them being able to move in the first of October. That's why she's been pushing so hard. Maybe I—we—can help out...without her knowing it, of course."

Teddy pretended to take that under serious consideration, but there was a suspicious twinkle in his eyes. "Maybe *we* could."

Elizabeth came out of the bedroom a short time later. "She fought the pill the doctor gave her as long as she could, but she's asleep now. I thought I'd use the time to go home and pack an overnight bag. I don't think she should be alone for the next day or so."

"Channing can stay, can't you, son?"

Son? Giles felt a rush of panic skip through him like a stone racing over the surface of a lake. But to his amazement, instead of protesting, he found himself agreeing with the older man.

"Yes, of course. Besides, my apartment is close. If I need anything, I can be there and back before she'd notice."

"See, dear?" Teddy put down his glass and picked up Elizabeth's clutch purse. Shoving it into her hands, he wheeled her around toward the door. "Everything's under control. We can keep our dinner engagement with the mayor and his wife knowing that Kate's in good hands."

"Father, have you no shame?"

To Giles's disappointment, Teddy's answer was lost in the slam of the door as he drew it shut behind them. He would have liked to hear how the old scoundrel got himself out of that one. Even more, he wanted to know how *he*—a reasonably intelligent man—was managing to get himself deeper and deeper into a quagmire of his own making.

He would do well to recheck the family Bible next time he went back to England, he told himself as he polished off the rest of his brandy. Grabbing up Teddy's snifter, he carried both to the kitchen sink. It had to be an abnormality in the genes, something that skipped generations.

Chances were if he dug deep enough, he would find a
great-great uncle or someone the family had sequestered
away from polite society for being slightly unhinged. And
at the rate of his regression, he brooded as he yanked off
his tie and slumped down into a chair, it wouldn't be long
before the men in white came to pay him a visit.

Hours later, Kate rose to consciousness feeling as though
she were riding a glass elevator up through dense fog.
Feeling came in degrees and with it the realization that her
hands hurt worse then ever and her tongue had swelled to
the size of her mattress. With a moan she pushed herself
onto her elbow.

A faint light streaked into her room from the partially
opened door. Liz, she thought affectionately. She hadn't
forgotten her long-ago confession about her fear of the
dark and had left a small light on in the kitchen.

Using it to guide her, she eased out from beneath the
bedspread and shuffled to the bathroom. Groping gin-
gerly for the bathroom light, she winced at the blinding
glare when she turned it on.

"Mmph," she mumbled, grimacing at her reflection in
the wall-length vanity mirror.

Whatever makeup she'd been wearing earlier this
morning—*whatever* morning—had since worn away,
leaving her looking like one of the ghouls on those Satur-
day-night late shows. Equally bad were her hair and
clothes. What she wouldn't give for a shower or a long
soak in the tub. But as she eyed her bandaged hands, she
knew she was going to have enough trouble getting a drink
of water.

Turning on the cold water tap was easier then she'd
hoped. Of course, her sister would have explained it was
because she never shut the things off properly to begin

with. Licking her lips with anticipation, she picked up the yellow plastic cup with both hands and stuck it under the slow stream of water.

Too thirsty to wait for the glass to fill completely, she greedily downed a half cup, then went back for a refill. It was as she was drinking the second cupful that she looked in the mirror and saw the reflection of the man entering her bedroom.

She screamed, the cup shot out of her hands like a Jupiter rocket and water came down with the density of a spring downpour. In the next instant light illuminated Giles's face and her legs gave beneath her. With a groan, she slumped down onto the white-and-yellow shag throw rug.

"Hells bells, Giles!" she wheezed, pressing the edge of her palms against her eyes. "You scared me clear into next month."

"Sorry." He crouched before her. "I heard you moving around in here and I wanted to see if you were all right."

"Well, next time send a telegram first. What are you doing here? Isn't it late?"

"Long after midnight. You've been out of it for nearly twelve hours. How do you feel?"

"How would you feel if you'd—" The words stuck in her throat as she looked up and found him very close and looking very comfortable. His hair, mussed from sleep, fell over his forehead, shadowing his sleep reddened eyes. His jaw was darkened by a night's growth of beard that made him look slightly barbarous. He'd stripped down to his white pants and against it, his tanned chest, dusted with an intriguing mat of black hair, looked very dark and more muscular than she would ever have imagined. "Oh, my," she breathed softly.

His slow grin grew to a wide slash of gleaming white teeth. "That's an extremely Victorian response, Miss Katherine. In this day and age one would think young women had become somewhat jaded to the sight of shirtless men."

Maybe, she thought, but none she'd seen had ever made her feel the things he did. "It's just that you look—different."

"So do you." With his finger, he traced the path of a droplet of water down her nose. His gaze moved downward over the silk shirt that was now plastered to her shoulders and breasts like a second layer of skin. The lace design on her bra was only slightly less beguiling as the demi-cut. "Not that I don't approve," he murmured, but out of necessity shifted his gaze. "How are the hands?"

Realizing that he'd almost made her forget about them, she glanced down. "They'd started to throb. I think that's what woke me."

"Dr. Quisenberry had some antibiotics sent over and a painkiller. Why don't we get you dried off and back into bed, and I'll get them."

Gently grasping her forearms, he helped her to her feet. Then he took one of the fluffy yellow towels off the rack and began to dab it over her face and hair. She hadn't been treated with so much care since she'd broken her wrist falling off her first horse. Leona had made her rice pudding with raisins and even added a touch of rum, and she'd held her in her arms while reading *Black Beauty*.

Kate closed her eyes and sighed with contentment. "Why did you stay?"

He paused momentarily, then slid the towel down to dry her throat. "Ask me an easier question."

"Okay, why didn't you go home?"

She was irresistible when she consciously flirted with him and, looping the towel around her neck, he drew her against him until they were nose to nose. "Because I couldn't bring myself to leave. I tried—at least I think I did—and the next thing I knew I was telling your father that I would stay to keep an eye on you."

"You'd better be careful. You're liable to put ideas in his head."

"He does well enough without any help from me." Unable to stop himself, he traced her delicate jawline with his thumbs. Like a kitten needing pampering, she arched her neck, asking for more. "You should go back to bed," he reminded her again.

"I know, and I'm making you wet. It can't be pleasant."

No, it wasn't pleasant. It was arousing. His body heat and hers were warming the wet silk and increasing his awareness of how little separated them. Already there was a knot of tension forming in the pit of his belly. If he kissed her as he longed to, it would grow, take control. For both their sakes, he couldn't let that happen.

"Get back into bed, Kate."

"I can't. Not in these wet things."

"Then change into—" Did she sleep in nightgowns or pajamas or *anything*? "—Something else," he said, nearly croaking. "I'll give you a few minutes and bring in the pills."

He withdrew the towel and hung it over the shower door to dry, congratulating himself for easing out of a potentially sticky situation. But when he turned back to find she was fumbling, albeit unsuccessfully, with the buttons of her shirt, he knew he'd been premature with the felicitations.

"Uh, Kate. Don't you think—"

She gave him a sheepish, hardly apologetic smile. "Looks like I need help again."

Why hadn't he thought about that? Why hadn't he realized those bandages would make it difficult for her to dress and undress herself? Elizabeth would have handled this so much better, he thought, his gaze centering to the pale arrow of flesh exposed by the one button she'd managed to wrestle open.

"Yes, well, why don't we move into here," he said, directing her by her elbow back into the dark bedroom, "and you can tell me where you keep your nighties."

Kate bit her lip to keep from laughing. She thought it very sweet that he was actually nervous, but *nighties*? Then she reminded herself that up until a few weeks ago, when she'd gone to Elizabeth's favorite boutique to buy that dress, her sleeping attire had consisted of oversize shirts and college football jerseys.

"Top right," she said, gesturing with her bandaged hand to the French-style oak dresser.

Giles opened the drawer and felt the knot inside him expand to twice its size. He had to be caught up in some kind of dream; this wasn't the lingerie drawer of the Kate Beaumont he thought he knew. Neatly folded stacks of silk, satin and lace gleamed up at him in the dim light like confections through a frost-glazed window. But it was the familiar glove, *his* glove resting on top that made his heart begin to pound, his blood begin to race.

With a not-quite-steady hand, he reached for a meringue-colored negligee. It slipped through his fingers as if it were melting, spreading the scent of her fragrance. He filled his lungs with it like a man who'd recognized he'd been outsmarted, accepted that he was outgunned, but planned to meet his end with style.

"Nice," he murmured, sliding the drawer closed and turning back to her. "And new."

Kate sat down on the bed because her legs were giving out again, though for a different reason. "As a rule, I don't care for shopping, so when I go, I have a tendency to splurge."

"I don't blame you." Giles draped the negligee over the bed and sat down facing her. "I'm the same way," he said, reaching for the first button on her blouse and then the next. "Have it done with, that's my motto."

"Oh, mine, too."

"Can you stand?"

"What?"

"Up." Bemused, she let him guide her to her feet and place her between his legs. "It's these fastenings," he murmured, undoing the waistband of her riding breeches.

She wasn't thinking about fastenings, she was thinking about how his warm breath caressed the bare skin at her waist. She could feel it clear through to her spine and down to her thighs, and she had to rest her hands on his shoulders for support. But she also couldn't resist lifting a hand to brush his hair off his forehead.

"It's as thick and as glossy as Zulu's mane."

And she was built like a thoroughbred, spare but what there was of her was prime. As he drew down the zipper of her breeches and slid them down her legs, he imagined them tightly wrapped around him.

"I'm better tempered."

"We'll see."

He lifted his eyes to hers. "You can sit down now."

She did—onto his lap.

"Kate." Heat shot into his loins and he had to take a steadying breath. "You need your rest."

She linked her arms around his neck. "I can rest later."

"You're sure this is what you want?" he asked, brushing her hair back over her shoulders, sliding his hands down her back and beneath her blouse.

"You don't sound like the man who, a few weeks ago, told me he wanted me."

"Want you?" Shifting his hands to her hips, he drew her more firmly into the cradle of his thighs so that she could feel the power of his need and he brushed his lips up and down the valley between her breasts. "I'm burning up with wanting you."

"Then since it's what we both want, why don't we stop tormenting each other."

In reply he pressed an ardent kiss on the inside curve of her left breast. No more torment, he agreed silently. But he wasn't going to rush this either. He'd wanted her too much, for what seemed too long not to prolong every delicious moment he could.

Her softness delighted him. As he traced his lips across the lace edge of her bra, he reached behind her to release the fastening, then drew it down her arms along with her blouse to explore more of her. Her skin was soft, but firm and sensitive to his slightest touch. He traced her delicate curves from shoulder to thigh with his fingertips and smiled when she couldn't hold back the shiver of anticipation.

"What do you want?" he whispered, rotating his thumbs in slow lazy circles, causing pleasure to ascend up her body in spurts and wisps and waves.

The higher they went the more Kate felt her breasts swell, until her nipples tightened with excitement. "Anything. Just don't stop touching me."

He didn't think he could if he wanted to, and he most definitely didn't want to. "Sweet, sweet Kate," he breathed drawing his parted lips along her inner arm, so close to where she needed him to touch her that he heard her breath catch and exit in a shaky sigh. The sound aroused him no less than her exquisite body did and, wanting to hear it again, he performed the same ministrations on her other arm, down the center of her chest. But his desire was generous not greedy, and only seconds later he rewarded her burgeoning breasts with a more intense invitation to mindless passion.

She hugged him closer, threw back her head and gave herself up to the dizzying pleasure. No one had ever brought her so far so quickly. No one had ever offered so much and asked for so little in return. As she arched against the deft exploration of his hands, she bit back a moan of ecstasy. "I wish I could touch you the same way. I wish—"

Before she could finish, he rolled back onto the bed and had her stretched over his hard length. "Use your body," he whispered against her lips. "Use your mouth. Do whatever you want. Just don't hold back the sounds, Kate. I want it all, as much as you do."

When she pressed her eager mouth to his, he felt as if a dam opened and a flood swept him away. He heard the roar, felt the sea pound in his ears and in his blood. It even tasted like her, and he drank greedily until his lungs threatened to burst with the need for air. But he wanted more; he wanted her to carry him to the edge. Shifting her more precisely over himself, he filled his hands with her slender hips and coaxed her into taking him there.

It was too much, yet not enough. He absorbed her shaky moans and arched his neck off the bed, then his shoulders as she sinuously trailed a path with her lips down his throat and over his chest. He didn't know which gave him the greater pleasure, her clever little tongue or her long hair as it followed like silky fingers. But when he slid his own fingers beneath the only scrap of clothing she wore and discovered the warm, sleek heart of her waiting for him, he knew he wouldn't bear to wait another moment.

Rolling her onto her back, he slid off the wisp of silk and lace. Her hands beat him to his belt, but he completed the task of stripping himself.

When he brought his body back against hers, he closed his eyes briefly, caught between agony and joy. His muscles rippled against the sleekness of hers, grew hot and damp. Pressing her deeper into the bedding he watched her eyes as her body accepted the slow invasion of his.

"Oh, how I want you," she whispered, wrapping her long legs around him.

"Katherine," he groaned and, crushing his mouth to hers, he gave himself up to oblivion.

Nine

He'd called her Katherine and she'd loved it.

The memory was one of the first to come to her when she awoke the next morning. The second was that she'd fallen asleep in his arms, never having gotten around to taking a painkiller, after all. But instead of making her smile, the thought caused her to frown.

Dear heaven, what had she done?

It had been good between them. Better than good; it had been incredible, an experience unlike any other. She could remember that first peak and how it seemed to go on and on, then when he'd aroused her again and, later, again. She'd found herself *needing* as much as wanting, and she wasn't sure how she felt about that. She wasn't sure of anything except that he was no longer in bed with her... and damn it all, that hurt.

The least he could have done was hang around this morning to say something. Not that she had any idea what she wanted to hear.

Then, beyond the bedroom door she heard a drawer open and shut, a faucet run. He was in the kitchen—making coffee from the way things sounded. But her relief and eagerness for a shot of caffeine lasted only a moment, only as long as it took her to think about what they were going to say to each other.

Knowing she wasn't going to be able to face anyone without at least having her hair combed and teeth brushed, she reached for the negligee that, like most of the bedding, had slipped to the floor. Dragging it on, she hurried to the bathroom.

Ten minutes later, when Giles walked in carrying the tray, he found the room empty. Setting the tray on the chest at the foot of the bed, he crossed over to the window to open the blinds. Deciding it made things too bright, he reclosed the blinds halfway. There was something to be said about subdued lighting when one was groping around for honesty, he decided.

"Kate? Breakfast," he called over his shoulder.

Within seconds he heard her fumbling with the doorknob, but before he could cross the room to help, she had the door open and was dashing for the bed. He experienced a sharp pang of desire as he watched pale silk and lace caress her body. When she tucked the sheet demurely beneath her arms, he was almost grateful. Here he was, supposedly taking care of her, and all he had on his mind was stripping her out of that thing and losing himself again in her intoxicating sweetness.

"Good morning," he murmured, concentrating on picking up the tray and setting it across her lap without spilling everything. "How do you feel?"

"Fine." The word came out as a dry whisper. She didn't know what looked better, him or the food. He was dressed in the same clothes he'd worn yesterday, but the shirt was merely tucked into his slacks, not buttoned, and it gave her a tantalizing view of the masculine chest that had intrigued her so last night. The tray was laden with everything from strawberries and cream to quiche and pigs in a blanket. "It looks like you went through a lot of trouble for me. I know none of that was in my refrigerator."

"I know a very grateful chef at the Omni."

"What did you do, promise to finance his own restaurant?"

"An intriguing thought—he'd make me a fortune. But no, it was more like promising him a feature in *Gourmet*."

Good grief, they sounded more like polite strangers bumping elbows in a buffet line than lovers. Kate dropped her gaze to the tray again. At least there was plenty there to keep her preoccupied. She felt like a child let loose on a shopping binge in a toy store and touched her tongue to her upper lip, wondering what to dig into first.

"How about some help," Giles said, unfolding the green linen napkin and spreading it across her lap. "What'll it be? Never mind. The quiche probably should be eaten while still warm, but if ever I saw a more deserving mouth for strawberries and cream . . ."

Kate's mouth was watering by the time he dipped the berry and lifted it to her lips. When he finally placed it between her teeth, she closed her eyes and bit it ravenously from the stem he held. The mingling flavors exploded in her mouth drawing a moan of pleasure from her.

Giles felt himself leaning close to lick the remaining juice from her lips and caught himself just in time. But not in time for Kate to miss seeing his withdrawal and the evasive shift of his eyes.

"Ready for another?" he asked gruffly. Maybe he needed to go slow on the berries. "Here how about tasting the quiche."

"I can do it."

"You'll get your bandages dirty."

"So they'll get dirty. That's no reason for you to feel obligated to hand feed me." Determined not to be a charity case, she reached for another berry, but he surprised her by brushing her hand away and shifting the whole tray out of her reach. "Hey! I've barely started on that."

"I think we'd better talk first."

"There's nothing to talk about."

He gave her a skeptical look and took a calming breath. "I'm handling this badly. Kate—"

"Look, Giles, breakfast in bed was a lovely gesture and last night was fine—all right, it was great," she amended when she saw his eyebrow arch familiarly. "But I hardly need an involved explanation about how you need your space right now. What we shared was done in mutual agreement. There were no strings attached."

"No? Then why can't I leave?"

"Am I stopping you?"

"I didn't say you were," he snapped.

"So what's the problem?" she asked just as testily.

"I'm terrified, all right!"

"Well, so am I!"

The silence that followed seemed to echo between them. They could see the truth of their words reflected in their eyes, replacing the wariness and the agitation. They could see something else, too... a need to understand. It was enough to allow Giles to reach for one of Kate's hands, lift it to his lips and place a tender kiss on her fingertips.

"I'm sorry. I was so caught up in my own thoughts, I didn't think what you might be feeling."

Kate glanced away as embarrassment replaced her anger. "When I awoke this morning, I didn't know whether I was more relieved or hurt that you weren't still in bed with me. It seems to capsulize my feelings pretty well—I don't know myself anymore. Not when I'm around you."

Giles nodded slowly. "I've always been able to walk away from people, relationships, almost anything."

"Me, too. Well, at least the men Daddy paraded past me."

"You've changed all that . . . and last night changed everything."

Kate closed her eyes. "We're not suited to one another. It would never work. You're the most traditional man I've ever met."

"The devil you say," he replied, almost laughing. "Me? I've been rejecting tradition since I was old enough to understand that Richard could be counted on to keep the family name honorable. *You're* the one who's bound by tradition."

"Me?" It was Kate's turn to look incredulous. "My nickname in school was 'Rebel.' I'm the family black sheep, always bucking the system, the first to question, the last to bend to the rule of the majority. I practically break out in hives at the thought of going to teas and socials. That's the kind of woman you need in your life."

"Thanks heaps. Shall I wish someone just as bland on you? How about a banker or estate lawyer?"

"Bite your tongue," she chuckled, scooping up a bit of cream from the bowl and after threatening to dab it on his nose, held it to his lips.

Laughing quietly, Giles caught her wrist and, careful of her bandages, licked her finger clean. He felt her pulse leap with the stroke of his tongue and saw awareness flicker in her eyes. His own thoughts shifted just as quickly.

"Ah, Kate..." He sighed, leaning closer to touch his lips to hers. "If I had a half an ounce of decency I'd beg you to kick me out of here. But all I can think of is laying you back against those pillows and kissing you senseless."

That was exactly what Kate wanted too. She didn't have any more answers than he did. All she knew was that she felt alive in his arms and complete in a way that was new and exciting. This couldn't work out for them; she was still convinced that they were all wrong for each other; but if she could have just a few more hours with him, maybe she could satisfy the hunger that sprang to life whenever he touched her.

"I can't be logical without a strong dose of caffeine first," she murmured, drawing the tips of her fingers through the dark hair matting his chest. "And I think the coffee's already cold. We can warm it up in the micro-wave—later."

Recognizing that with her desire stayed very close to the surface, he accepted the sudden lunge of his heart against his ribs and freed himself from his shirt. Sinking his hands into her hair, he drew her up and kissed her as he'd been longing to since he'd forced himself out of her bed. "Later," he agreed thickly, lowering her back to the pillows. "And maybe it would be best if we take this slowly...so we don't make any mistakes."

As he claimed her silk-covered breast, Kate closed her eyes in ecstasy. "Oh, please...make it very, very slow."

They slept afterward and salvaged what they could of their breakfast. Then when his conscience got the best of him, Giles made Kate take a nap alone. By late afternoon she was rested enough to join him in the living room as he poured through several newspapers and the briefcase of work he'd gone to pick up at his apartment while she'd been sleeping. Though he'd obviously showered and changed and looked content to work in her place, Kate wondered that he wouldn't prefer being at his own apartment.

"I don't need a baby-sitter," she told him as she slumped down beside him on the sofa and began wrestling with the banana she'd grabbed from the fruit bowl. "If you have things that need your attention elsewhere, you needn't put them off for me. I can manage on my own."

"About as well as you can peel that?" he asked, tossing away a stock report and snatching the fruit from her. He proceeded to peel the banana, then fed it to her. They'd already gone through this before when he'd told her of Quisenberry's instructions. "Face it, my sweet. You're grounded for the next several days, and I'm staying to make sure you behave. Granted, your absence will make it tougher on Maxwell and the others, but they'll figure something out. The thing that's not going to happen is your landing in a hospital because you've run yourself into the ground."

Kate gulped down a mouthful of banana while eyeing him dolefully. "You know what? Your English charm is deceiving—you'd make a great dictator...and—" she frowned as he dropped the empty banana peel on top of the read papers "—I'm still hungry."

"Little Philistine." He shook his head at the picture she made in her short blue robe that did nothing to hide her slenderness. "You must have the most incredible metabolism."

"When I was born, Leona had to supplement my mother's nursing with a bottle. She said I grabbed at it like a shoat and haven't slowed down since."

Though he knew it was dangerous to learn too much about her, Giles found himself wanting to know. "Your mother passed away when you were still quite young, didn't she?"

"Mmm. It was difficult for all of us. She was so gentle and kind, and she—slipped away from us so quietly, like vapor." She smiled sadly. "I remember her hands the most. She had the softest, palest hands."

"I barely remember my mother," Giles replied, unaware that he'd taken *her* hand. "She died when I was two, in a train accident. She'd been coming home from a Christmas shopping expedition in London."

Kate could picture him as a young boy sitting at a window and waiting for what would never be. Her eyes filled with unexpected tears. "How sad," she whispered.

Tempted to tell her more, Giles found himself withdrawing, rising to go to the window and look outside. "It was a long time ago, and the rest of my childhood memories are good ones. We had enormous fun, thanks to my father, who was a colorful character, and Nanny. Can't leave her out. Richard used to call her the dragon, but that's because he was jealous of the way we got on."

Kate could imagine. She didn't think there was a woman alive who was safe from him. "Is she still living?"

"She's indomitable. She raised Richard's brood and now she's starting a new dynasty on Big Salt. It's a private island in the Caribbean," he explained upon seeing her raised eyebrows. "O'Keefe and his family live there."

"It sounds like a ski resort in Utah."

"At the time he washed up on its beaches, I suppose O'Keefe wished it were—you see, his boat went down in a storm. The island's doctor nursed him back to health. Poor darling, all Laura got for her troubles was marriage to the tyrant."

Kate smiled at his droll humor, almost grateful for it, but at the same time her curiosity and need to understand was piqued. "Tell me why you left home?"

"It's quite simple really. Curse of the second son and all that. My father passed away just before I graduated from Oxford and, being the eldest, Richard naturally inherited the estate and title. He wanted me to take over managing the family's ceramic-ware business— You *are* familiar with China by Channing?" He watched her cover her mouth with her bandaged hand in an attempt not to laugh and gave her a mock look of scorn. "No? My dear, we only supply the best hotels in Europe. At any rate, I didn't want the bloody ceramic business or the department stores. Heaven knows I'm no dairy farmer, and Richard wouldn't hear of turning the place into a horse ranch. So what was left for me? I had no choice but to seek my fortune elsewhere."

This was far more interesting than what what she'd read in the papers. Kate picked up a pillow and hugged it to her. "Did you really make your first million backing a movie?"

"My first million *outside* the family trust, and technically it was during a game of chemin de fer on the Riviera. I was playing a Hollywood producer—now there's a character—and if I hadn't cleaned out old Rodney, he wouldn't have needed a backer for his low-budget film. Strange how fate works out. If I hadn't been driving across the States to check on my investment, I'd never have met O'Keefe, and if I'd never have bought Orion—" he turned back to her "—I'd never have met you."

"Maybe you'd have been better off," Kate murmured, feeling his probing gaze.

"Maybe we both would."

That stung and Kate tossed away the pillow and scrambled to her feet. "I was serious about being hungry. How about pasta? I know of this great place that delivers and—Giles!''

He couldn't stand it. The look of hurt on her face was too much. As cautious as he was feeling, he couldn't stay away from her and in two strides he was across the room, swinging her into his arms. ''Kiss me,'' he demanded, already seeking her mouth with his. ''I need you, Kate. Forgive me, but it's the one thing I *am* certain of. I need you.''

Desperation. Panic. She recognized them because she felt them herself. Oh, yes, and need, too, she thought, unhesitatingly wrapping her arms around his neck. Dear God, what lunacy this was all evolving into. But how could she resist it? At the least they could give each other oblivion. How many other people even found that?

''Remind me to call Quisenberry in the morning and ask him for the name of a good shrink,'' she whispered against his lips as he carried her back into her bedroom.

''Ask if we could get a group discount. We'll both go.''

Kate gave languoring her best effort. She knew she wasn't the most patient person, but by Thursday she decided even a couch potato would have been bored silly with being cooped up in her apartment. Giles tried to help. He brought over video movies and magazines every night. However, he'd been called away to Miami this morning, and the prospect of spending another day with nothing more than her own company to entertain her, along with facing their first night apart since Saturday, had her stripping leaves off her Boston fern by late morning.

When she heard the knocking at the door, she knew that even if it was only her mailman delivering a package, she was going to invite him in for iced tea and a slice of the cheesecake Giles had brought home with dinner last night.

But better than the mailman, it was her sister she spotted through the door's peephole and, giving a whoop of delight, she wrestled with the chain and bolt.

"Well, that answers my first question," Elizabeth chuckled as Kate hugged her and dragged her inside. "I'd called Quisenberry and he said to keep the visits to a minimum, but I knew he'd forgotten what you were like when you were confined to your bed with the measles."

"This is worse. I'd actually been staring at the walls and playing with the idea of painting a mural."

"Not a good idea unless you've heard that they're planning to turn this place into a preschool afterward. No, don't look at me like a whipped puppy—you forget, I've seen you draw."

"I think I have a good eye for color coordination."

"Mmm . . . think of it, little green-and-yellow stick people strung across the walls, or maybe you should try green and salmon, they're still very much in vogue. Good grief, what have you done to that fern?"

"I wanted to make a salad for lunch and realized I was out of lettuce," Kate drawled, following her sister into the kitchen where she set the sack she was carrying onto the counter. "What did you bring? Yum, I smell Leona's chicken. Oh, good, the paper. Giles hasn't let me near one since Sunday, he says it's a negative influence on recuperation. Can you believe it?"

Elizabeth pursed her lips as she slid off the bolero jacket of her peach-colored suit and handed it to Kate to hang over a bar stool. "And how *is* the recuperation going?"

Kate held up her hands. She'd stopped wearing the bandages Tuesday, and though the skin was still pink, it was no longer as tender as it had been.

"And the relationship?"

"Oh, God. Did you bring a suitcase? This could take a while."

Elizabeth hugged her before indicating the bar stool. "Sit. I may not have any answers for you, but I have a feeling if you don't talk it out soon, you're going to drive yourself crazy."

While Elizabeth unpacked the sack and portioned the contents of the meal she'd brought onto two plates, Kate filled her in on what had happened over the past few days. She left nothing out, though she knew it was the most intimate conversation they'd shared in their lives.

Ten minutes later, when they were sitting by the glass dinette table looking out over the complex's pool and tennis courts, she finished as breathlessly as she'd started. Elizabeth looked out the window at the few people who were relaxing around the pool. The tennis courts were empty; it was already too hot for playing.

"Funny how you tend to think clever people should be able to be more sensible about life and love than anyone else." Elizabeth laid down her salad fork to reach over and touch her sister's hand. "You *are* in love with him, Kate. Can you at least accept that?"

Kate had to put down her glass of Chablis, the mere thought made her hands shake. "Yes. Especially when he's gone, like now, and I think how it'll be tomorrow before he's back in town and I wonder if he's safe, if he's thinking about me, if he's not driving himself too hard."

"So what's the problem?"

"I don't want to turn into Little Mary Homemaker. I don't want to lose my independence, my right to work at what I choose, befriend whom I choose, express my opinion when, where and how I choose...." She saw her sister cover a smile and sighed. "It's not funny, Liz."

"Kate, do you really think anyone could ever change you?"

"The other day he mentioned liking marinated artichoke hearts. Liz, you know how I detest those things, but I phoned out for some so I could serve them with dinner and actually let him *feed* me one."

Elizabeth burst into laughter. "I'm sorry, sweetheart. I can't help it. Don't you understand that happens to everybody. Love means compromising—some compromises are easier than others, yet they're not going to change the real you. In fact you might like discovering new dimensions in yourself."

Common sense told Kate that her sister was right, but it didn't make the butterflies in her stomach go away. "Well, it doesn't matter one way or another. Giles feels the same way I do."

Elizabeth glanced up from meticulously peeling the skin off Leona's deep-fried chicken breast. Humor lightened her blue-gray eyes to an almost Wedgewood shade and her cheeks brightened to match the peach in her polka-dotted blouse. "Is that why his robe is on the back of your bathroom door? I couldn't miss it when I was in there washing my hands. You'd better hide it from Dad if he ever pops over. He might have pushed me out of here Saturday when Giles said he'd stay to look after you—but I don't think he had quite this in mind."

Kate had taken a crunchy bite of a chicken leg and was forced to gulp it down. "Good grief, he's not a prude."

"No, but he does have two sets of standards—one for his darling daughters and one for the rest of the world. Do you know the night before my wedding he asked me if he should send Leona up to talk to me about—are you ready?—*things*."

"He thought you were still a virgin!"

"I *was* a virgin. But I didn't need anyone to explain the birds and the bees to me."

Kate almost dropped her drumstick. Elizabeth had been just short of twenty-one when she and Daniel married. They'd dated on and off all through college. Even if *they* hadn't slept together, there was still—

"Are you serious?" she asked, nearly whispering.

"Scout's honor, and you know Daniel was always the perfect gentleman. He never pushed it."

"Well, don't tell me Morgan didn't." Seeing her sister's shock and subsequent withdrawal, Kate leaned across the table, her look entreating. "Come on, Liz, we're sisters."

"I did *not* sleep with Morgan Deveroux."

"But you wanted to, right?"

"Kate, you should go into some sort of investigative work. You're relentless."

She'd actually thought about being an investigative reporter. Between wanting to be a glider pilot and a professional figure skater. She'd quickly decided that the tedium of the job would outweigh the excitement.

She also decided to try a different approach with her sister. "Have you seen him since I told you he's back?"

With a long-suffering sigh, Elizabeth stopped playing around with the cherry tomato in her salad bowl and put down her fork. "No, I haven't, nor do I expect to. Morgan's situation might have improved since the days when he worked at Meadowbrook, but that doesn't mean we're automatically going to be circulating in the same social circles."

"Elizabeth Jeanette, that's the most snobbish thing I've ever heard you say. Why shouldn't you?"

"I didn't mean it in that way," Elizabeth said quickly, clearly embarrassed. "I meant—oh, bother. Morgan once made it very clear what he thought of me and 'my kind,' as he put it. Now can we please change the subject?"

"Okay, okay." Kate topped off both their glasses. "I was only trying to mend fences and help the poor guy out."

She changed the subject and the rest of their visit went smoothly, but Kate's thoughts returned to their conversation and Liz's touchiness about Morgan later that afternoon. After making her way through a few sections of the newspaper, she spotted a picture of her sister and father at last week's dinner party with the mayor.

Elizabeth looked ravishing in her black gown and very much at home in the mayor's mansion. She might look as though that was what she wanted out of life, but Kate wasn't convinced as she studied the black-and-white photo. Maybe her sister understood the theory behind relationships and compromise, but in the end Elizabeth was no better at it than she was.

Compromising . . . she turned the page. Hadn't Giles already shown her shades of that himself? All week now Rusty had been accusing her of driving him crazy when she called to check how things were going at the office and renovation sight; but being a hands-on person himself, Giles understood her need to keep tabs on how the project was going. Hadn't he supported her need to do that despite Quisenberry's orders?

A smile lit her face as she spotted the picture of her in Giles's arms after the horse show. About to go get the scissors to cut it out, she spotted another. It was of Giles in shirtsleeves and a hard hat, pointing out of camera range and talking to— Kate's mouth fell open as she focused on the copy.

As if Beaumont Center developer Giles Channing weren't busy enough, he's generously offering his time and talents to the renovation of the Parker Building, recently placed in trust to ABA for use by the city's less fortunate. With him is ABA senior director Rusty Maxwell, also helping in the project.

"Also?" Kate's hurt turned to red-hot anger. Of all the sneaky, low-down tricks. What a fool she'd been. And to think Elizabeth had actually succeeded in getting her to start thinking, *hoping . . .* No, she wouldn't think of that now. The only truth that mattered was that he'd been using her all along. And Rusty had been in on it. "Well, this is one phone call he won't be able to worm his way out of taking," she muttered, reaching for the phone.

Was she going to be surprised, Giles thought just after midnight as he tossed his suitcase and briefcase into the Jaguar at the airport and climbed in. It had all but killed him, yet he'd delegated, crammed and rescheduled his way into catching the last flight to Atlanta. Kate wasn't expecting him until tomorrow, but he hadn't been in Miami more than a few hours when he'd realized he simply didn't want to spend the night away from her. Not yet. Maybe not ever again.

He was falling in love. Him. The last of the holdouts.

It hit him when he was cruising at thirty thousand feet and he'd looked up at the flight attendant who was refilling his coffee cup. Only his eyes had played tricks on him and all he saw was Kate as she'd looked when he'd said goodbye. Now all he could think of was the way she would greet him when she found him at her door. It did wonders to push away the fatigue and the caffeine headache drilling into his temples.

He would have preferred to take things more slowly—he was still overwhelmed by what had happened between them—but he should have known better than to think it was possible with Kate. From the moment she'd welcomed him into her bed—perhaps it went all the way back to the beginning—there'd been a part of him that had known he didn't stand a chance. He'd been walking around bedazzled ever since.

There were no lights on in her apartment when he arrived at her complex and parked the car. But it didn't matter, he had her extra key. Thinking about how good it would feel to slip into bed beside her and cuddle up to her warm body had his heart almost skipping by the time he climbed the stairs and slipped the key into the dead bolt.

He hadn't remembered the chain.

Damn, he thought, peering through the narrow gap and seeing the living room slightly illuminated by a small kitchen light. He tried to slip his hand in and undo the chain, but naturally it was impossible. His hand was too large.

"Kate?" he called in a loud whisper. Even that made him wince and he glanced over his shoulder, feeling like a fool. All he needed was someone spotting him. They would think he was trying to break in and call the police. "Kate, it's me. Wake up!"

She did...she had the moment she heard the key go into the lock, and she was already scrambling out of bed. But even though she thought she recognized Giles's voice, she grabbed her tennis racket from behind her bedroom door. Just in case, she assured herself, gripping it firmly.

"Kate!"

"Shh!" she whispered just as loudly when she peered out at him. "You're going to wake up the whole building."

"Sorry. I forgot about the chain. Open the door, love."

"Right after it snows in Bora Bora."

"What?"

"You're supposed to be in Miami. What happened? Did that traitor, ex-friend of mine call you and tip you off that you'd been found out?"

"I wanted to surprise—" Giles shook his head, certain that he was missing something important. "Kate, what's wrong?"

"Oh, that's good. Play innocent until the very end. Well, let me tell you something, Giles Channing," she said, shoving the tennis racket through the door and poking him in the chest. "I'm on to you. I saw the picture in the paper of you and Rusty, and I think what you've done stinks!"

"Picture of me and—oh, hell." He raked his hand through his hair and took a deep breath. He should have known she would see that. "Open the door, Kate. I can explain everything."

"Ha!"

"Katherine," he warned, his voice growing louder, "if you don't open this bloody door, I'll knock it in. Then we can *both* be featured on tomorrow's front page—after the press catches us being bailed out of jail for disturbing the peace. Now open it!"

She did, but only after assuring herself that she was doing so because any scene that transpired was a personal one and nothing she wanted to share with the public at large. Tossing the racket onto a nearby chair, she closed the door and unlatched the chain. As soon as she reopened the door to him, Giles pushed his way inside.

"Don't make yourself comfortable," she snapped, watching him set his briefcase and suitcase by the hallway leading to the bedrooms. "You're not staying."

He turned slowly. Patience, he reminded himself. It was just a misunderstanding. Once he explained, she would see that.

He even managed a smile when he noticed how adorable she looked. She was wearing something that looked like a painter's smock, the neckline low and ending in a large white satin bow, the hem brushing her thighs. It was far more demure than the other nightwear she'd tantalized him with over the past several nights; except that where she was standing he could see the outline of her body through the smock, and that only reminded him of how much he wanted her.

Then he saw the condemnation in her eyes and he had to take a deep, stabilizing breath to suppress a new and different surge of panic.

"Are you going to let me tell you what happened, or are you going to judge me on circumstantial evidence?" he asked grimly.

It wasn't fair. He had no right to turn it around to make it sound as if she was being unreasonable. She'd seen the photo. She'd called Rusty. He hadn't denied Giles had taken over for her at the site. Oh, he'd tried to explain, excuse himself, as well. But she'd felt so betrayed, felt so angry, she'd hung up before she embarrassed herself by bursting into tears.

"You lied to me," she said, lifting her chin. "Part of the agreement my father made with Reverend Mitchell and his people was that you weren't going to use them to make yourselves look good with the media."

"And I thoroughly intended to keep my word. I didn't *ask* that reporter to show up at the Parker Building."

"The point is *you* shouldn't have been there, either!" She laughed bitterly. "What a fool I've been. All this time I've been driving myself batty trying to follow the doctor's orders and trying to please you, thinking with your hectic schedule and concerns about Beaumont Center you didn't need the added preoccupation of worrying about my health. But the only thing you've been worrying about is getting caught, because you've been sneaking around behind my back taking over *my* project so you can take credit with the media."

Giles stared at her incredulously. "Listen to yourself. *Your* project? Is this the same woman who stood before the TV cameras and insisted she was simply one small soldier in a very committed army of volunteers?" He needed a drink.

As he turned away from her, Kate grabbed the sleeve of his gray suit jacket. "I said it and I meant it. But this supervisory job was important to me. Just once I wanted to show my father and Rusty that I was more than a pretty face, that I could do more than administrate. You of all people should understand the need to feel you've accomplished something, to look at a building that you helped create and see tangible proof that you've made a difference."

"I do," he replied wearily. But he had to look away from the tears he saw shimmering in her eyes. If he looked, he would end up forgetting everything but the need to provide comfort, and that would be a mistake as critical as the one she'd made. "That's why, after Quisenberry told you that you needed a week's rest, I went to introduce myself to Rusty Maxwell and to figure out a way we could keep the project going until you could take over again. I juggled my own schedule to make the time, Kate. I asked my own people to wait. All for you. Then some silly reporter jumps to the wrong conclusions and you buy it without even giving me the slightest benefit of the doubt."

He'd done all that for her. Why hadn't she seen it? She felt sick to her stomach. "Giles, I had no idea—"

"Maybe not, but couldn't you have waited and asked? Damn it all, Kate, if we can't even trust one another, what are we doing together?"

The awful truth in his words was more harsh than a blow. A tear slipped free from her brimming eyes and she quickly brushed it away, then another. He was right. She'd let him down. How could she? Why hadn't she listened to her *heart*? She'd said she'd wanted people to take her seriously; instead she'd behaved like the brat Morgan had teasingly called her.

"I'm so sorry," she whispered. "It's so rare to find anyone who doesn't expect something in return for a donation or a good turn these days. Giles, I know it's no excuse, but I've been burned so often that I suppose I've grown suspicious of people and their motives."

"I'm not people."

No. He was the man she'd confessed being in love with, and look how she'd expressed her feelings for him. That and the realization that he had every right to walk out of her life—was, in fact, heading toward his things—made the tears flow even faster.

Giles was gripping the handles of his cases when he heard her muffle a sob. He'd never been very good around crying women, but hearing Kate ripped him apart. With a muttered oath, he dropped his things. With two long strides he crossed the room, hauled her into his arms and crushed her to him.

"God, stop. Please, don't," he muttered, stroking her hair. "Kate, you don't know what you're doing to me. I can't fight tears."

"I don't want you to fight it. I want you to forgive m-me." She clung to him, absorbing his warmth as much as his strength. "Giles, I'm so ashamed. Can you forgive me? It won't happen again, I promise."

"At least not until it snows in Bora Bora, eh?" It was impossible not to laugh. "Ah, Kate. You can no more make a promise like that than you can change who you are. But at the same time, I suppose I should have told you what Rusty and I were trying to do for you."

"No, it was a lovely surprise and I'm very grateful for it." She pressed a kiss against his throat and another near his ear, enjoying the fresh masculine scent that clung to his skin.

Giles could feel the last of his annoyance melt away, and in its place came the wanting that always stayed very close to the surface whenever he touched Kate. Did he really believe he could have walked away from her? He closed his eyes, absorbing the feel of her lips and ran his hands over the silk that only enhanced her softness.

"Did you really finish early?" she asked, massaging the tension she felt in his shoulders and neck muscles.

"No. But when I realized I wasn't concentrating worth a damn, I delegated all the work and caught the last flight home. God, that feels good."

The word "home" wasn't lost on her and she smiled in the darkness.

"You're so tight. Let me get you that drink."

"No. You," he said, kissing away the last of her tears. "I only want you."

There was forgiveness in his caresses, and that ever-present need. Feeling as if her heart would burst with relief and happiness, Kate wrapped her arms more tightly around him and gave him the passion he seemed to crave. Never, she vowed to herself, never again would she risk losing what they shared.

"Come with me," she whispered against his lips.

Taking his hands, she drew him down the hallway to her bedroom. Once there, she released him only to slide off his jacket. As he reached for his tie, she covered his hands with hers.

"No, let me take care of you for a change."

With deft movements, she slipped the blue-and-silver patterned tie from its knot and then started on the buttons of his shirt. She could feel his heart beating forcefully against the backs of her fingers and, when she was able, she parted the material to press her lips to his chest.

Giles slid his fingers deep into her hair, silently urging her to deepen the kiss, to explore him to her heart's content. But as her tongue brushed over his nipple, he realized how fragile his grip on control really was tonight, and with a moan of regret he tightened his hands to hold her still.

"Kate, I think I'm way ahead of you tonight."

"All right." With a final caress, she gently pushed him onto the bed. "Then why don't you take off your shoes while I get . . . comfortable."

There was only the bow and three buttons to her shirt. Before Giles could do more than slip out of his loafers, she was letting the sheer silk slide down her arms and pressing him all the way back onto the rumpled sheets. The languid, erotic glide of her body against his was more than he could bear, and something dark and not quite civilized took hold of him.

With one hand gripping a handful of her hair and the other sliding low to press her hard against his aching loins, he crushed her mouth to his for a devouring kiss. He wanted everything and more. He wanted to absorb her into himself and in doing that obliterate the memory of what they'd almost done to each other.

Together they struggled with his belt and the last barriers that separated them, and then she was guiding him into her. The speed, the heat, it was almost too much, but they couldn't stop. When Kate began to rock against him, the urgency grew and grew until it threatened to sever their link with sanity. He wanted nothing less.

"Kate...harder..." Giles rasped. His pale eyes glittered fiercely in the dim light and he gripped her hips with encouragement. "Kate!"

She felt it start, too, and vowed that this was a fire that would never die between them, even if he felt compelled to leave her. Kissing him deeply, she drank in his moan as her body absorbed his pleasure.

Ten

Look at the little show-off.'' Kate chuckled watching Moonflower as she hopped over and around higher thatches of grass in the private pen she shared with Gypsy. "She thinks she's already a jumper like her momma." In fact, the filly was a miniature replica of the mare, except that she had a white mark on her nose in the shape of the vine-growing flower.

"She seems to be a superior foal, I'll give you that," Jackson said, resting his forearms on the railing beside Kate. "Barely more than a month old and her legs are as straight as a two-monther. Promising chest and rump formation, too. It'll be interesting to see her at three to five months."

Kate shook her head, but grinned. "You're such a pessimist."

"I'm judging her with my head, not my heart like some people around here." But when he glanced over at Kate,

172   KISS ME KATE

his hazel eyes were amused. He considered her hyacinth-blue wrap-around dress. "I thought you were going to work with Zulu in the ring today. The state fair isn't that far off, you know."

Kate glanced at her watch. "I did earlier, while you were in the north pasture cutting up the tree that fell on the fence. Quite a storm last night. Did you see any other signs of damage?"

"The usual, leaves and branches messing up the trails and such, but nothing serious." He caught her glancing over her shoulder and sighed. "Are you itching to go somewhere? Don't think you need to hang around here to entertain me."

"Don't grumble just because you weren't around to add your two cents to my performance in the ring. I'm expecting Giles. He's supposed to fly in from Miami this morning and we're going to lunch." She checked her watch again. "I guess the plane must have been delayed. He should have been here almost an hour ago."

"Hmph. Well, some of us have more important things to do than stand around and waste time daydreaming," Jackson muttered and shuffled away toward the stables.

Kate repressed the impulse to reply to that, even though she knew the only thing he did on Saturdays after the morning feedings and seeing the helpers had chores was to find a sunny spot on his porch and rock himself to sleep. She turned back to watch Moonflower return to her mother to nurse. Her thoughts, however, drifted miles away.

She really was beginning to worry about Giles. True, it wasn't uncommon for him to get tied up in meetings, but usually he phoned if he knew he was going to be late. It was one of the many ways he tried to show consideration to her . . . her way of showing consideration to him.

Three weeks, she mused, closing her eyes and lifting her face to the mid-September sun. It had been three weeks since she'd made that awful mistake, and in every moment they'd shared since she felt their feelings for each other deepening. But just as they had that night, they remained silent in actually expressing them.

Realizing she was just depressing herself even more, she pushed away the brooding thoughts and began walking back toward the house. She was halfway there when she saw the sleek Jaguar round the drive and head toward her. With a sigh of relief, she broke into a smile and waved.

"Lord, you're a delicious sight," Giles murmured the moment he pulled up beside her. "Come here and give a starving man a kiss."

He needn't have asked, she was already ducking toward the window. It had only been two days, she reminded herself, but the separation had seemed so much longer. "I missed you," she whispered against his lips before kissing him again.

"You couldn't have missed me half as much as I missed you. Why don't you hop in and I'll tell you all about it."

"Let me go inside and get my purse first."

"Get in and I'll drive you back." He dropped his admiring gaze to the pretty-but-flimsy high-heeled sandals she was wearing. "You shouldn't be walking around this uneven ground in those anyway. It's a wonder you haven't sprained your ankle."

More than happy to comply, she rounded the car and slid in beside him. "It's your fault," she teased, giving his slate-blue tie a tug. "I was trying to kill time waiting for you. I was worried, you know." There wasn't, she decided, anyone like him. He brought her laughter and desire simultaneously and, with a soft sound of pleasure, she slipped her arms around his neck and gave him the mind-drugging kiss he'd asked for.

"Better," he murmured after several long moments. "I might pull through now. Maybe. You don't know how much I wanted one of those. When someone invents a way to send a kiss through a fax machine, they're going to make a billion."

"Well, it wasn't me who said you should go off to Miami. But how did things go at headquarters?"

Giles slowly eased the car around and headed it back down the driveway. "Not bad. The project in Puerto Rico is still up in the air, but we won the Dallas job."

"Congratulations," Kate replied, hoping she sounded suitably happy for him. She was happy *and* proud, only she couldn't help worrying about how much more time he would have to spend away from her.

"And how has your project been going since I've been gone?" he asked, breaking into her thoughts.

"Fine. We'll finish ahead of schedule, thanks to your help. But I decided I wasn't cut out to tackle these big renovation jobs and I turned down Rusty's offer to—Giles, where are you going?" she asked as he continued past the house and headed down the tree-lined driveway.

"You'll see."

"I told you I needed my purse."

"No, you don't." At the main road he turned toward Atlanta and quickly accelerated. "You do, however, need to buckle up."

Kate did, but gave him a suspicious look. "What's going on? I thought you'd promised to buy me lunch?"

"The woman is forever thinking of her stomach," he complained, but smiled as he concentrated on the road.

"The woman is starving."

He reached over to lace his fingers through hers and carried her hand to his lips. "I promise to buy you the biggest steak-and-lobster dinner to be had—later. Satisfied?"

"Do I have a choice?"

"Now what kind of kidnapping would this be if I gave you one?"

Kate knew better than to comment further, but her curiosity about where they were going hadn't been satisfied. Giles didn't do anything to relieve it, either, choosing instead to talk about his flight, the weather and every trivial subject he could think of...until he turned into a driveway several miles down the road.

Kate looked from the overgrown grass to the For Sale sign attached to the locked wrought-iron gate to Giles, who was reaching into the pocket of the suit jacket he'd hung up behind her seat. "This is the Fairchild estate. When did it go on the market?"

"Yesterday, from what the real-estate agent told me when I went back to the city to pick up the key." He got out and unlocked the gate, leaving Kate to stare. "Apparently they've decided it requires too much upkeep and they're moving to their summer cottage on the coast," he said upon returning. "Ever been inside?"

"No. Have you?"

"Of course. That's why I'm late. I admit when I heard he was an artist, I had my reservations about taking a closer look—you know how eccentric artists can be—but I was pleasantly surprised."

As he eased the sports car around the potholes worn into the paved drive, Kate nodded, but remained completely confused. What did that mean, 'taking a closer look'? Was Giles now planning to venture into renovating estates? A moment later she spotted the house through the natural screen of noble beech trees that had yet to turn the brilliant shades of autumn, and her attention focused on it.

Not just a house, she realized a moment later as they drove around one of the tall stone walls—it was more like a compound. Between the house and barn was a graveled courtyard with a pool and fountain. The house itself looked austere with its tall windows, their shutters providing the only decoration or privacy, yet Kate couldn't deny its primitive charm.

"I feel like we've stepped back in time and landed in some old European winery," she told Giles as they exited the car and looked around.

"Fairchild had it designed after a place he visited in the south of France near Provence. He preferred keeping the windows bare of shrubs and draperies because he needed the light to work, but I thought Italian cypress would look good against these walls, and some sort of vine there." Grabbing her hand, he led her to the front door. "Come look inside. There's an open-air terrace that was made for alfresco dining."

At first Kate felt like an intruder walking through the expressively decorated rooms, but within minutes she overcame that and could appreciate Giles's attraction. The house wasn't like anything she'd seen in the area, and she finally understood the whispers she'd heard when she was young of the odd artist and his wife who lived like recluses. Older now, she respected and admired their choice to be different.

"It's a marvelous place," she told Giles, glancing over her shoulder as he led her back outside and across to the barn. "But if you're thinking of buying it and reselling for a profit, don't change too much. The primitive style is half the charm. Of course, you'd want to talk Fairchild into leaving a few of his paintings. The one over the fireplace of that field of wildflowers is glorious.''

"Sell it? I want to live in it.''

Kate came to an abrupt halt just inside the opened double doors.

"What?'' he asked, smiling at her incredulous expression. "Is that so hard to believe?''

Yes, she thought, trying to take it all in. Wasn't this the man who only a few months ago told her he wanted no complications in his life, no ties?

"Do you realize what you're talking about?'' she asked, turning away so that he wouldn't see the hope in her eyes. "This isn't like an apartment or condo. Something like this means responsibility.''

"Upkeep.''

"Roots.''

"Someday to be followed by little roots.''

"*What?*''

"Come out of the sun, darling,'' Giles drawled, drawing her farther into the barn. "I think it's making you obtuse.''

"Obtuse my fanny. What about Dallas...and Puerto Rico...and all those other places where you're going to build? What about all those warnings you gave me not to get involved with you because one day you'd leave me? What about—''

"Katherine. Do you love me?''

"Yes, damn it!''

"Then say you'll marry me and then shut up.''

Kate didn't consider herself brilliant, but she wasn't slow either. With a squeal of joy, she flung herself into his arms and covered his face with random kisses, the last landing very accurately, very fervently on his lips.

"Tell me," she demanded, her voice breathless, her eyes sparkling as she scanned his face adoringly. "I want to hear you say it."

His smile was indulgent. "With or without poetry?"

"Without."

"I love you Kate."

"Oh—that's nice," she whispered, closing her eyes as if she were tasting the words. "Now with."

Giles's chest shook with laughter. "You're crazy."

"No, just greedy. I want to experience it all with you. I didn't think this was going to happen, and I'm only beginning to realize that I've been waiting so long for someone of my own to love who would love me back."

"I do understand, darling," he murmured, framing her face between his hands. "Perhaps I wasn't looking for this when I first met you, but I can't walk away from it now that I've found it. Be my love, sweet Kate, and I'll share my life, my heart and everything I am with you."

"Yes, yes, yes!" she whispered, crushing her lips to his.

Giles eagerly wrapped his arms around her and deepened the kiss to a full exploration that soon left him breathing unevenly. She would always do this to him, he realized, feeling his body respond to the nearness of hers.

"Umm...Kate?" His intent was unmistakable when he edged her back to a soft pile of hay warmed by the sun peeking in through a window. Kissing her again, he coaxed her down, smiling approvingly as she began to loosen his tie. "Have I told you that you have wonderfully talented hands?"

"No, but go ahead. It'll keep my mind off thinking a snake or mouse could pop out of this stuff at any moment."

"And ruin my big seduction scene? They wouldn't dare. But just in case—" he traced a path of kisses down the side of her neck, untied the bow at her waist and slipped his hand inside her dress to claim one silk-covered breast "—I'll do my best to keep you preoccupied."

Kate fumbled with one of the buttons on his shirt and then another as Giles began to stroke his thumb across her sensitive nipple. When he lowered his head to suckle her through the sheer material of her chemise, she gave up and restlessly yanked, popping off the last button and sending it into the hay. "That will definitely—preoccupy me," she sighed, letting her eyes drift closed.

"Mmm...but try to remember that I have to be able to walk out of here looking reasonably presentable."

Kate's laughter filled the shadow-filled barn, echoing back at him and sounding more mischievous and young than he'd ever heard it. It made him feel younger, too. He hadn't expected love to do that to him, turn him into a boy again, fill him with hope and dreams. He had everything a man could possibly want, but somehow she was giving him the promise of even more. The wonder of it caused an exquisite ache deep in his chest.

Ever so naturally, their playful lovemaking turned tender, and wonderfully slow. There were times when they'd made love, that he thought her passion would ignite him into flames, when he needed the fast, fierce pace to assuage his sense of urgency. But he knew that he would always cherish this languid pace most. Nourished by affection as much as desire, it continued as steadily, as serenely as the ribbon of a stream that ran out back beyond the house.

The hay and their bodies heated, intensifying the musky scents and murmured words of encouragement. Kate watched the sunlight turn Giles's tautly muscled back the color of molten bronze. Lovingly she smoothed her hands over him again and again, erasing the memory of the hours they'd spent apart and the fears that had come with them. When he finished undressing her and himself, she thought she couldn't want him more than at that moment. Then he stroked his fingers down and into her and she was reminded that there was no end to the amount of pleasure he could bring her.

His name was a sigh on her lips. He cut the word off by claiming her mouth and making her melt with his tongue and hands. Only when he was certain she was as ready for him as he was for her, did he shift between her legs and take final possession.

Even then the tenderness remained, though he intensified their movements by sliding his hands down to lift her hips to the slow thrust of his. Hearing him say her name, she opened her eyes to find him watching her.

"Tell me you love me," he whispered, accepting that his heart, like his future, lay forever in her hands.

She wrapped her arms even tighter around him. "Always. No matter what."

Smiling at her fervent promise, he brought them to an endless release that was all the more sublime because it was shared in love.

Giles thought he could happily have gone to sleep. The last two days had been manic, the nights not much better since he was discovering that he didn't sleep well away from Kate. But energetic bundle that she was, within minutes she was mischievously drawing a blade of hay around the rim of his ear.

"This is so much nicer than an engagement ring," she mused aloud.

Not at all fooled, Giles lifted one eyelid. "If you can wait long enough for us to get to the car, you can check the other pocket in my jacket." Instantly Kate was sitting up and sorting through her clothes. "Little mercenary," he chuckled, tugging her back so that she sprawled across his chest.

"Is there really a ring?"

"Mmm-hmm. I had it expressed over from England and waiting for me when I flew in this morning."

"You mean this was all planned?"

"Well, not quite all, no," he murmured dryly. "Er—the ring *is* a family heirloom." He ran his finger down the length of her pert nose. "I expect you to be properly impressed."

Kate gave him a smacking kiss. "You're so sexy when you get snobbish."

When they'd dressed, reexplored the house and grounds and returned to the car, Kate held up her hand to examine the ring Giles had placed on her finger. It was an emerald-cut diamond bordered by three rows of smaller diamonds on either side. What was incredible was that it fit as though made for her.

"It's lovely, Giles, and enormous. I'll be afraid to wear it anywhere."

"That's the idea. It's supposed to remind you at all times that you belong to me now."

She threw her arms around his neck and kissed him. "And you belong to me. Thank you, darling, I love it. Now let's go show Liz and Daddy."

It was a good hour later when they burst through the front door. Giles dryly suggested Kate go upstairs and brush the remaining bits of hay out of her hair before they faced her family, then meet him back in the study. Catching a glimpse of herself in the foyer mirror, she laughingly agreed and raced up the stairs.

Elizabeth was just coming out of her bedroom as Kate ran down the hallway. She snatched her sister's hand and pulled her into her own room.

Torn between amusement and annoyance, Elizabeth plucked a strand of hay out of Kate's hair and shook her head. "For heaven's sake, where have you been? You look as though you've been rolling around in the—" Suddenly she found herself staring at the ring. "Is that what I think it is?"

"It was his maternal grandmother's. Isn't it incredible?"

"I hope it comes with guards."

"I know what you mean. Liz, I feel like I've stepped into some kind of fairy tale. He loves me! I'm going to be Mrs. Giles Quinn Channing."

Elizabeth's eyes filled with tears and she hugged Kate close. "Oh, sweetheart, I'm so happy for you. I don't even have to ask if this is what you want." She sat Kate down before her vanity and, picking up a brush, began to comb out her hair. "Tell me everything. What date have you picked?"

"A date...I guess we haven't yet."

"That sounds like you."

"But I want you to be my matron of honor."

"I'd be honored. Then it's to be a church wedding?"

Kate gave her sister a mild look in the mirror. "Do you think Daddy would miss out on an opportunity to strut down the aisle? Besides, Giles says that his brother and sister-in-law will want to come."

"The Earl! I'll have to phone the papers...and I'd better talk to Leona about getting more help."

Kate rolled her eyes. "Liz, his name is Richard. I wonder how he'd take to being called Rick?" she added thoughtfully.

"Oh, God." Elizabeth waved away the image that projected. "Just tell me how Dad's taking this. You know, despite everything, I don't know if he's ready to lose his baby.''

"Giles is down in his study now. I'd better get down there." She jumped to her feet and gave her sister another hug, then remembered something. "By the way, we ran into Morgan down the road. I invited him to the wedding and guess what? He said he'd come."

All the pleasure went out of Elizabeth's eyes and she sank down on the vanity stool. "Oh, Katherine. How could you!"

"Channing! So you're back. Good to see you," Teddy said, entering his study to find the younger man gazing out one of the tall windows. "I was just trying to figure out what happened to Kate. She said she was going to have lunch with you today, but I didn't hear you come in. Pour you a drink?"

Giles accepted and asked for a bourbon and water. "How have things been going at the complex?"

"I can't believe she's finally taking shape," Teddy said, poured two drinks and handed one to Giles before lifting his glass in salute. "If the weather holds, they should be able to start working on the interior by Thanksgiving. You know, I've never watched for hurricanes the way I am this year. So, tell me, how was Miami?"

"Fine. I've asked her to marry me."

"Good, good. I'm fond of the place myself. A bit more hectic than— What did you say?"

"I've asked Kate to marry me. She's said yes."

Teddy stared at him dumbfounded for a moment then slapped his thigh and burst into a deep belly laugh.

Giles lifted an eyebrow and smiled dryly. "I assume that means we have your approval?"

"Approval? My boy, I'm delighted. Speechless, but delighted. How did you manage it? No, never mind. As long as it's settled and she's happy. She *is* happy?"

"We both are, thank you."

"Well, that's marvelous, just marvelous." Teddy crossed the room and shook hands with his future son-in-law. "I know you could do it if anyone could. And I'll keep my word, you know," he added, touching his glass to Giles's. "The moment you put a ring on my girl's finger, half the complex is yours."

As if a strong wind had just rushed through the room the door to the study slammed shut. The force shook the windows and rattled the genuine Confederate sword that was mounted on the wall. But it wasn't wind that had done it, nor was it wind that made Giles stiffen and Teddy's face turn gray. It was Kate, who'd heard everything and was now standing there watching them.

In her eyes were unmistakable blue flames of temper.

Eleven

———

Damn,'' Giles muttered, casting a look of frustration toward Teddy. ''Now look what you've done.''

''Hush, son. I'll take care of this,'' Teddy replied thrusting out his chest. ''Katherine Anne, it's a fine day that a daughter of mine eavesdrops on a private conversation.''

''Oh, hell,'' Giles groaned. Setting his glass down, he crossed over to Kate. ''All right, I won't deny it sounds bad. But if you'll just hear me out, nothing is the way it sounds. I'll admit your father did initially come to me with a proposition.''

''Katy, dear, I had nothing but your best interests at heart,'' Teddy explained in his own defense.

''But I turned him down,'' Giles concluded. ''I told him that I'd seen too many marriages of convenience in my family to ever want to bend to that tradition myself, that if I was going to ask a woman to marry me, it would be for love and nothing less. You have to believe that, Kate. My God, I'd forgotten all about that foolish offer. I want you for my wife because I love you and for no other reason."

Kate had been listening quietly, staring down at the blue-and-gold patterned rug as if she didn't trust herself to look elsewhere. But finally she raised her eyes to consider her father, who cleared his throat and took a quick sip of his bourbon. Then she turned to Giles and, breaking into a serene smile, lightly kissed his cheek.

"I know that, darling. But thank you for telling me anyway."

As Teddy choked on his drink and pounded his fist against his chest, Giles exhaled in relief and drew Kate into his arms.

"You mean that's it?" her father blustered. "He just says so and you believe him?"

"He's the man I'm going to marry," she replied, calmly, gazing at the man who held her. "If I can't trust him, who can I trust?"

"Ahem. Yes, well..."

"As for you, you old reprobate." Kate narrowed her eyes and, easing herself out of Giles's arms, took a step toward her father. But in the next instant she burst into laughter at his meek expression and extended her arms for a hug. "I forgive you. However, in the future kindly leave your meddling nose out of my love life."

"Aw, now Kate...it worked out well, didn't it?"

"No thanks to you."

Ignoring the sarcasm, Teddy patted her back, then un-abashedly wiped away the tears that filled his eyes. "Well, isn't this a fine day. You know you had me worried for a minute there. I can't tell you how pleased I am."

"Mmm. I can imagine."

"We have to celebrate. I'll go tell Leona to fix something special for dinner and ice down a couple bottles of champagne. Then we can talk. There's a lot to plan."

"Later, Daddy." Kate took Giles's hand and led him to the door. "We have some business to take care of first."

"Wait a minute. I think we should discuss living arrangements as soon as possible. There's plenty of room here, you know."

"Too late. We're off to buy the Fairchild estate."

"That crazy artist's cave? What the hell are you going to do there?"

"Make little roots," Kate called over her shoulder just before she closed the door behind them.

"*What?*"

Giles let her lead him until they were out on the front porch and then he tugged her into his arms. "You," he murmured, touching his lips to hers, "are a dangerous woman. When you first came in, I was sure you were going to reach for your father's saber and have a go at both of us."

Kate traced his lower lip with her finger. "Keep that in mind for the future, sir. Just because you've discovered my weakness for you doesn't mean you'll always get off so easily. Now why don't we go return that key and negotiate a deal they can't refuse?"

"Just one more indulgence," he asked with a slow smile. "Then I swear I'll never abuse the weakness again."

Kate sighed theatrically. "Uh-huh. What is it?"

"Give us a kiss, Kate."

Laughing, she slipped her arms around his neck, her eyes shining with love. "Oh, my dearest lord," she murmured, "abuse *that* weakness all you want."

*   *   *   *   *

SILHOUETTE Desire™

COMING NEXT MONTH

#571 SLOW BURN—Mary Lynn Baxter
Lance O'Brien's kidnapping was over in a moment. Marnie Lee was left to deal with the aftershock—and with Lance's father, Tate O'Brien, a most enticing captor himself.

#572 LOOK BEYOND THE DREAM—Noelle Berry McCue
Erin Kennedy was surprised to land a job at a California health club—and when she met her blue-blooded boss, Logan Sinclair, she knew her wildest dreams had come true.

#573 TEMPORARY HONEYMOON—Katherine Granger
Overefficient Martha Simmons was just doing her job when she agreed to temporarily marry her boss, Jake Molloy. But once they said their ''I dos,'' she hoped permanent love would follow.

#574 HOT ON HER TRAIL—Jean Barrett
Beth Holland was hiking the Appalachian Trail to save precious land from destruction. Opposition came in the form of sexy Brian McArdle.... Could he sidetrack Beth *and* walk away with her heart?

#575 SMILES—Cathie Linz
Classy dentist Laura Peters was haunted by fears of failure—until she met roguish Sam Mitchell, who taught her to believe in herself and to smile her doubts away.

#576 SHOWDOWN—Nancy Martin
Manhattan attorney Amelia Daniels came to Montana to find her runaway daughter and ended up in the arms of June's *Man of the Month*, charming, irascible cowboy Ross Fletcher!

AVAILABLE NOW:

#565 TIME ENOUGH FOR LOVE
Carole Buck

#566 BABE IN THE WOODS
Jackie Merritt

#567 TAKE THE RISK
Susan Meier

#568 MIXED MESSAGES
Linda Lael Miller

**#569 WRONG ADDRESS,
RIGHT PLACE**
Lass Small

#570 KISS ME KATE
Helen Myers

Take 4 bestselling love stories FREE

Plus get a FREE surprise gift!

A collector's edition hardcover romance FREE!

SILHOUETTE'S

Diamond Jubilee Collection

Annette Broadrick
Ann Major
Dixie Browning

To celebrate its 10th Anniversary, Silhouette Romance is offering a limited edition, hardcover anthology of three early Silhouette Romance titles written by three of your favorite authors!

These titles—CIRCUMSTANTIAL EVIDENCE by Annette Broadrick, WILD LADY by Ann Major and ISLAND ON THE HILL by Dixie Browning—were first published in the early 1980s. This special collection will not be sold in retail stores and is only available through this exclusive offer:

Look for details in all Silhouette series published in June, July and August.

FREE-1